TRAIN✦FLIGHT

THE BIRTH OF SALVATION

ELIZABETH NEWTON

Imprint: Salt and Light Press

All Rights Reserved
First Edition

Newton, Elizabeth (author)
Train Flight
Book 2: The Birth of Salvation
ISBN 978-1-7640008-1-9

For J.

BOOK TWO

This story is the second of the Train Flight series. It can be read by itself, but it is also part of the ongoing adventures of Evie and Paulo on the Train with the Captain.

Others in the series so far:
1. Moon Man

The Engine Room

TRAIN RULES:

1. Stay with Captain
2. Don't wander off
3. Let Captain do the talking
4. Don't ask too many unnecessary questions
5. Always make sure your shoelaces are tied up tight.

CHAPTER

1

TIME CRASH

There is a man who owns a train. Not many people know what this Train really is, but perhaps *you* know. Perhaps you've read about this Train before. Or perhaps you've even adventured on board... in which case... perhaps we've met. In the past. Or even the future...

Anyway, I assume you're reading this book in the present, and so in case you haven't travelled on or read about the Train, I'll let you in on the secret... It travels in time and space.

But this is far from the most exciting part.

You see, this story is not really about this man, but another Man. Except *this* Man was not a man in this story, but a Baby, and you might be wondering why I'm using a capital letter for this Man. One reason is for pure convenience. When you read 'Man' with a capital 'M', you'll know I'm not talking about the first man with the train, but the other Man. This Man was not of this world, and when the man met the Man, it changed the man's life. The man wanted to learn everything about the Man and to help others discover the Man too, which brings me to the second reason I've given that Man a capital 'M'.

This particular Man is very special. So special that creation did some very peculiar things when He was born. So special that wind and waves obey Him, as well as the suns and planets of the universe. In fact, He spoke them into existence in the first place. So you can see how that might deserve a capital letter.

Now I hope you're following correctly and don't think that the *man* did all this. It was the Man... who was a Baby. Which I know must sound confusing, so I'll just tell the story and you'll see for yourself, shall I?

Unfortunately, this story begins with some unpleasantness. And I don't wish to confuse you, but it starts with two men. And neither of them are the two m/Men I've already mentioned.♣ *These* two men were extremely unpleasant. One man was much more unpleasant than the other man but fortunately that man is not in this story for more than a page, so for now, all we have to worry about is the other man who *wasn't* as unpleasant, (although, he had enough unpleasantness for my liking.)

For one, at this moment he was throwing a chair across the room. At least, he did it in his mind. But he could have been killed on the spot for doing a thing like that. So instead, Mallory roared, "You can't leave me here!"

A gaunt, shadowy figure with a tangle of black hair (the other man) stood in the corner. His calm, sly voice spoke in mock-sympathy, "Aww, you thought you were coming with me. That's cute. Through thick and thin and all that?"

"But we're partners!"

"*Were* partners, old man. Turns out it doesn't suit me anymore." His smooth whispers were calm as a frozen sea. The monotonous humming of the device in the gloomy underground room had more feeling than his farewell.

♣ There are women in this story too, in case you were wondering. Just bear with me.

3

Mallory had never yelled at him before, but now, he held nothing back. "But I stuck beside you all these years! Longer than your *precious Beth!*"

The man's smile momentarily faltered, but was back again in a heartbeat. "Mallory, you've known all along this thing would only have enough power for one person. You might be able to rustle up something else. I wish you luck." His smug smile told Mallory that he wished no such thing. He sniggered out a quiet, wheezy cough.

"You won't get far in your current state," Mallory said coldly.

"I'll figure something out. Goodbye old friend."

"I'm no *friend* of yours."

"Aww Mallory, you're breaking my *heart*. Well, cheerio." And the man was gone, as if the musty air had silently swallowed him up.

Mallory swore at the empty space. The wooden chair finally took flight and smashed into shards and splinters against the cold stone wall. He shouted until his throat was screaming in pain and the veins in his neck bulged. He turned and punched the wall beside him, wincing in pain and regret afterwards.

All of a sudden, he was alone. In a strange world, in a strange place. Strange people all around. Above him. He didn't belong here.

It wasn't until a chilly October evening eight years later, when he had finally finished with all the bits and pieces of leftover tech. Down in that dugout, underground room, which was his secret from the world, Mallory stood back from his very own re-creation, and said with a maniacal smile, "It is ready."

In the empty, silent void of the time vortex, a steam train was whirling out of control. There had been a loud **THUD** which had the passengers frantically searching for answers.

"Meteor shower?" suggested Paulo Vistar, wobbling off his balance.*

"Collision with another satellite?" shouted Evie Bamford, hoping desperately that it wasn't.♦

"Can't be either of those things," said the Captain♠ over all the grinding and rattling. "There's nothing showing on the radar screen." He was leaping from one control to another. But no amount

---

* A young man from a planet called Serothia. He looked about seventeen in Earth years, (which is thirty-two in Serothian years).

♦ Thirteen-year-old Evie was from Australia on Earth, and flying towards a giant satellite was how her first adventure with the Captain had begun.

♠ who was the man.

of leaping, grasping, turning, pushing or pulling did any good. "My controls aren't responding," he told the others. "And this reading makes no sense!"

"What's it say?" Evie shouted.

"It says we're going back in time. And really, really fast! I can't stop it! **2019. 1992. 1805. 1634. 1211. 321...** You'd better get down on the floor, quick! I don't know when we're going to land, but it's certainly going to be a big crash!"

Now, every time traveller knows that a time crash is much more dangerous and unpredictable than a plain and simple physical crash. So after the Captain had made one last hopeless attempt to regain control, all three of them were crouched down on the floor of the carriage room, braced for impact.

Everything stopped.
There was a long... silent... wait.

"...Was that it?" said Evie, afraid to open her eyes.

The Captain opened one of his and glanced around at his all-in-one-piece Train. He opened his other eye and began to pick himself up. As usual, he left Evie in suspense by not replying and looked over the controls in silence. The front of the Train's engine room was a wall of taps, wheels, buttons, and lights. The room looked just like an old steam train cabin underneath a layer of futuristic spacecraft equipment. He ran a hand over the control deck, the way you might pet a friendly, injured dog.

Evie and Paulo stood up slowly. "Ev-everything alright?" Evie asked timidly.

"I'm sorry," the Captain finally said in his distinctive English accent. He was still frowning down at his controls. "I was supposed to be taking you home, and now you're far from it.

"Where are we?" asked Paulo, plainly.

The Captain, leaning back against the control deck with his arms folded, *answered* plainly, "We're in the year 4 B.C."

CHAPTER

ANGELS WE HAVE HEARD ON HIGH

Evie and Paulo trailed through the little adjoining carriage room behind the Captain. When they reached the outer door, Paulo hesitated. "Is it... necessary to leave the Train?"

"Are you kidding?" said Evie. "We're more than two thousand years back in time. This has got to be the most exciting thing that's ever happened to me. Of *course* it's necessary!" She felt a swelling whirl of nervousness rush through her as her foot landed on the ground outside. She wasn't even born yet, and she'd just made a footprint in the grass. "Hang on," she said. "What planet are we on?"

"Well, at least the Train got that part right," said the Captain, "we're on Earth."

"This is *Earth*?" asked Paulo, excitement beginning to get in the way of his nervousness.

"...in 4 B.C." Evie was in a daze. The silvery moonlight shone off her dark, wide eyes. "What's B.C. mean again?"

"Before Christ. A Romanian monk decided to estimate when Christ was born and start counting the years from then. So then all the years *before* then were counted too, but backwards."

"So this is four years before this Christ person was born?" said Paulo.

The Captain smiled distantly, "Yes, this Christ person. Although now they think the monk got it slightly wrong, but only by a few years."

"Brrr, it's cold," Evie said rubbing her arms up and down. "*Where* on Earth are we?"

"Couldn't get a precise reading," said the Captain, "but somewhere in Western Asia..."

"How is it that we can't see your spaceship, Captain?" Paulo asked.

"It's the paint," the Captain said.

"It's not invisible," Evie added. "You can actually see its surface."

"The paint causes an optical illusion, and your eyes see whatever they expect to see *behind* the Train. There's nothing but countryside out here and so your eyes fill the big gap where the Train is and tell you to see more countryside."

"I know what your next question is," Evie said with a smile. "and it's because the Captain wears those special driving goggle things, so that he can see it whenever he wants to."

"That's ingenious," said Paulo. "The perfect hiding place, anywhere you go."

"It doesn't stop people bumping into it though," said the Captain dryly.

Paulo smiled. "Before, what I meant by 'necessary' though was... well... could there be anything dangerous around?"

The Captain shrugged. "Well, *something* pulled the Train here; it wasn't a time crash. So I'm not sure *what* we'll find. And even if we don't find answers, we're still stuck until I can fix the controls."

"Well I'm glad we're stuck for now," Evie said.

"Yes, it seems you got your wish," said the Captain. "Could there be any reason in particular you're so eager *not* to go home just yet?"

"Well, you have a space and time travelling *train, der!*"

"So there's absolutely *no* other reason?"

Evie glanced down, guiltily. "You mean the whole *cheating-on-my-maths-test* thing."

"You won't be owning up about it anytime soon like you said you wanted to."

"I still want to! It's just..."

"She's glad of the extra time to consider what she'll say," suggested Paulo.

"Exactly!" said Evie starting to wander. "And being here, is just... I mean... I'm in *history!*"

"Ah, remember rule number two?" said the Captain.

"Don't wander off, yes."

"And rule number one for that matter."

"Stay with you, yes I remember."

"That applies to you too Paulo. We all stay close, alright?"

"Anyway," added Evie, "it's dead quiet out here in these fields or whatever they are. There can't be anyone around for miles."

"Hello?!" called a voice less than a mile away. "Who goes there?"

The three spun around to face where the voice had come from. They couldn't see anyone at first.

They must be on the other side of the Train, the Captain thought, bending his upper body over sideways to see beyond it.

There were two men in the silvery light of the moon, coming up a hill towards them.* Towards the Train. The Captain quickly jogged around to the

---

* These are another two completely different men. Sorry to confuse you.

12

other side, saving the approaching men a painful, embarrassing and highly confusing experience.

"There, straight ahead," one man said.

The Captain put his hands in his pockets and smiled cordially. "Good evening."

"I knew I heard voices..." the other man said.

Evie and Paulo appeared behind the Captain.

"Only... a moment ago, I could only see one of you. How the eyes play tricks."

"*I'll* say," smiled the Captain.

The travellers noticed the men's clothes. They wore simple hide boots, long ragged robes that were tied around the waist with cords, thick head scarfs, and cloaks made of unspun wool on their shoulders.

"What are you doing all the way out here?" one of them asked.

"Are you shepherds from a neighbouring field?" asked the other one.

Evie was about to answer, but the Captain quickly got in before her (after mouthing, "Rule number three.") "Er, well, I suppose you could say that we're from a sort-of neighbouring field, yes."

Rule number three was all about the Captain doing the talking. But the men were clearly looking questionably at Evelyn. She supposed that girl shepherds were not really a thing around here.

"Oh, this is Evelyn," the Captain interjected.

13

"She was lost... and she's trailing along with us until we can take her home."

"Where are your sheep?" asked one of the men.

"Sheep?"

Evie wondered whether the Captain was going to be able to whip out some sheep from out of his pocket like he did with most of his tools and peculiar gadgets.

The Captain was disheartened that it seemed he was going to have to whip out an actual fib. "They're lost."

"All of them?" the man said with alarm.

"All of them, yes. We'd lost one... er, hadn't we, Paulo, so we went to look for it... unsuccessfully of course, and when we came back, all the rest were gone too."

Evie bit her lips together, suppressing a chuckle. "Oh dear. That's awful."

"Are you hungry or anything?" said the other shepherd, who looked a little younger. "We have more than enough for ourselves."

"That's very generous of you, but actually, we're alright for food for a while."♣

_____

♣ As it happens, it was only about thirty minutes ago that they ate like kings at a very posh restaurant on Serothia.

14

"I'm Zacchaeus," said the older shepherd, "and this is Daniel. Why don't you come and rest with us? We're camping just over this hill. Continue your search after daybreak."

The Captain didn't want to delay his search but he knew that Zacchaeus was talking about sheep, not answers for why the Train was here. "That's very kind of you. I'm known as the Captain, this is my... fellow shepherd, Paulo, and as you know, this is Evelyn."

As the five of them started walking down the hill, Zaccheaus said awkwardly, "May I comment... your clothes seem very... well, I've never seen such garments. Where do you come from?"

The Captain was wearing brown trousers, a white shirt, a dull blue knitted waistcoat and a long dark trench coat over the top. He looked a bit like a 1930s car enthusiast when he wore his driving goggles and leather train-driver's cap. Evelyn was still wearing her jeans and black and white sandshoes. She had on a pink t-shirt and a white hooded jacket.✦ Paulo still had on his long-sleeve, sky-blue overalls which was his uniform on board the Serothian satellite.

"I suppose we do look rather different, don't

✦ which had in fact saved her life recently.

we," the Captain said.

The group came over the crest of the hill and came across a large huddle of sheep. "There they are," Daniel said. "They're a good flock. Something must have really spooked your sheep for them to wander off so far."

"Well it only takes one doesn't it," the Captain said. "And they all follow. Just like... well... sheep."

Evie had to cover another smile. It was like those times she was with her friends and her dad at the same time. And her dad would *speak*.

In the quiet moment that followed, Daniel's gentle, curious voice asked, "What's that?"

The others looked and saw that a glow of light was moving along the horizon line of another hill in the distance. It shone brighter and bigger every second, getting closer. The Captain narrowed his eyes. He wondered if it was a clue about why the Train had been pulled here. But then, as the glow crested over the hill, the shepherds and the travellers realised it was a horse. Gleaming white and galloping across the countryside, heading straight towards them. But it was its rider who was shining brighter than a full moon. He was at least seven-foot tall, broad, and strong, wearing gleaming plate mail. He looked quite literally like a knight in shining armour, only he wore no helmet, and they saw that his eyes were piercing golden lights. As he came closer, they had to shield their eyes. Their skin glowed and the grass gleamed as though it was daytime. Evelyn's heart raced, Paulo was frozen on the spot, and the Captain... every hair on his arms stood on end.

When the horse was right upon them, it stood on its hind legs and waved its front hooves in the air, whinnying loudly. The sheep backed away, nervously bleating. The rider looked down on them, and their hearts boomed inside their chests. They felt so puny cowering there, beneath him. But his face was kind, and when he spoke, his voice was smooth, deep and calm like an ancient mountain.

"Do not be afraid," he said. "I bring you good news of great joy that will be for all people."

Evie's heart jolted, wrenched upwards and swam around and around. She knew those words... She clutched her chest with her hand to make sure her heart was still in there.

The Captain straightened to try and look up again. His heart stirred wonderfully as he locked eyes with *the angel*. For he now knew that *that's* what this fearsome being was.

"Today in the town of David," the rider continued, "a Saviour has been born to you. He is Christ the Lord." He stared down at the five

17

dumbfounded faces gazing up at him and, with excitement, was quick to reveal more. "This will be a sign to you. You will find a baby wrapped in cloths and lying in a manger."

"Jesus," Evelyn let slip from her mouth. The rider looked right at her. Her stomach jumped. She thought she was going to be in trouble, but then... he smiled, and then a great company of angels, all huge and all with enormous wings appeared all over the hillside – some on the ground, some in the air! It was as though the sky had ripped apart; the radiant, blinding light was everywhere. Then the most beautiful sound emanated from them. Words. A Melody. They were singing!

Glory to God in the highest,
and on Earth peace to those on
whom His favour rests!

Their song was like fire and water at the same time. It trickled out of their mouths like a graceful stream, yet it withheld so much power, like something was about to erupt. Then, as quickly as it had all happened, the multitude of angels vanished upwards, leaving the one on the horse gazing down at them with his magnificent, piercing eyes. As he held the reins of the excited horse, his face gave another friendly smile. "What are you waiting for? Go! Go and find Him!" Then he reared the horse, and it galloped away, leaving the fields shrouded in night again.

CHAPTER

WONDER OF WONDERS

They stared into the night, unable to speak or move for a while. It was Daniel who finally spoke. "Let's go to Bethlehem to see this thing that's happened, that the Lord has told us about!"

"The *Lord* brought you this message?" asked Paulo. "But... why? And what's a... *saviour*?"

Zacchaeus answered, "The Saviour that's been promised!" He turned to Daniel, "Could it be?"

Paulo looked blank. The Captain said to him quietly, "*Saviour* is one of His names here. You wanted to learn more about Him... interesting we landed here..."

"Quickly, let's go," Daniel said. "I don't want to wait. The angel said it was the Christ!"

"Christ?" asked Paulo. "The one that monk..."

The Captain subtly placed a finger on his lips.

"Have you not heard the writings of the prophets?" said Zacchaeus. He was already collecting their gear and rounding up all the sheep. He got out some of their spare clothing. "Here, put these on. You'll blend in more."

"Wait, we're coming *with* you?" Evie said.

"Of course, why not! There's no time to lose."

"How far is David from here?" asked Paulo.

"The *town* of David," said the Captain. "That'd be Bethlehem."

"My family lives there," said Zacchaeus. "It's only a few miles west."

Evie was slipping a heavy robe over her shoulders, her heart racing. *This can't be real. This can't happen...* She sidled up to the Captain and asked quietly, "Is this really happening?"

"I think it is," he replied with a dazed smile. His crystal blue eyes were shining like shattered glass.

Evie had never seen his face so astounded and... nervous? Could he be nervous? She stared up at him. "We're going to see Jesus? *Actual* Jesus?"

"Right, everybody ready?" Zacchaeus said.

"I hope they won't mind us leaving a whole flock of sheep nearby," Daniel was saying later as they were walking along.

"I'm sure they won't," said the Captain. "There'll probably be other animals around anyway."

"What makes you say that?"

"Well..." said the Captain, carefully, "the angel said we'd find the Baby in a manger. That's what animals eat out of. Maybe they're in some kind of... animal place."

Evie pursed her lips into a private smile.

"Why do you think *we've* been told to go see Him?" said Daniel.

"I don't know," said Zacchaeus. "I can't think of anyone lower than a shepherd. Could it be a mistake?"

The Captain had his own private smile, "Did that angel look like the kind of creature who makes mistakes?"

Evie kept shaking her head, staring at the passing grass beneath her. *This has to be against the laws of time or something. I don't exist yet and I'm going to be there at... the Nativity Scene. That's in the Bible! How can I be in the Bible?*

"Are you alright Evelyn?" the Captain said suddenly, falling into step beside her.

"Yes," she said carelessly. "Everything's alright

'cause... this is just a dream. I'm just dreaming. I must have fallen asleep on the Train. Or maybe in James's car on the way to Summer Camp.♣ And the whole Captain-and-Train thing is a dream too. All of it. That makes much more sense actually."

The Captain just smiled.

"That angel looked at me like he knew me."

"He probably does."

Evie stared ahead, thinking. "I'm not actually. *Okay*, that is. I mean, I'm going to be a shepherd. I'm one of the shepherds, in the Bible, I'm *one* of them."

"I know. Bananas isn't it?"

"But it... it's wrong isn't it? I'll feel like an imposter."

"I know what you mean. But nothing happens that God doesn't know about. There's no place you can be that isn't where you're supposed to be. Well that's what John and Paul thought anyway."

"Are they saints or something?"

"Beatles."

"Beatles? ...Oh, your favourite band. Got it. But I mean... I just don't feel..."

"You don't think you're worthy. Like Zac and

♣ James was Evie's big brother. Just before Evie met the Captain, they had been on their way to a youth group Summer Camp.

24

Dan over there, you think it's a mistake."

Evie stared at the passing ground again.

"Well, you're *not* worthy. No one is. That's the crazy thing." He leaned down towards her and added with a playful smile, "But you are."

"But how can I be? I don't even know Him. Not... *personally* like everyone says I should."

"*I* don't know everything about Him."

"But, like... I have so much I don't know. And just don't get. Like... why did He even have to die?"

"Shh! Shh! Don't spoil the twist."

Her mouth curled up a little, but it quickly flattened again. "I just... People keep talking to me about it, but I just don't see how I fit in."

"Feels like more of a story than real life?"

"Yeah I guess so."

"Well I hate to state the obvious, but Bethlehem lies ahead," he pointed in front of them. "And here you are. In real life."

"I know, which makes it all the more *weird*."

He laughed loudly. "Weird is *wonderful!* You'll be fine! I'm right here with you. Come on, let's catch up to the others."

They soon fell into step behind Zacchaeus, Daniel and Paulo.

"Stray one," Zacchaeus said, and Daniel chased after one of the sheep that had started to wander away from the flock. He put his arms out wide and sidestepped around it, clapping his hands together, until it trotted back into the huddle of sheep. Daniel came back with news. "Hey, just over this crest, there are the lights of an inn. Bethlehem lies beyond."

"We'll see if we can rest at the inn for a short while," said Zacchaeus. "They might know something about the Baby."

Paulo asked the Captain in a hushed voice, "Why are we looking for a baby? Aren't we supposed to be working out what brought the Train here?"

"Patience Paulo. Just wait and see. Who knows? The two things might be connected."

"Mmm?"

"Not everything has a *scientific* explanation..."

"Do we have enough coin for an inn-stop?" said Daniel doubtfully. "And we'd have to take turns sitting with the sheep outside."

The Captain reached into one of his many pockets and brought out some round pieces of silver. "I have some money here if you need it. But I have a strange feeling they'll be full."

"Full?" said Zacchaeus. "Surely not this inn, so set apart from the town. They probably don't get much business around here."

"Sorry, there's no room," said the inn-keeper.

Evie pursed her lips to supress yet another giggle.

"Look, I know we look poor," said Zachaeus, "but we *can* pay you. And it's only for a short rest."

"It's not that sir," said the inn-keeper. "It's just that with the census and everything we're completely full up. We've not a room in sight! Not a bare space to hang your sandals, no place to rest your head, no room to swing a chicken, we're up to our necks in paying guests! I had to turn a young couple away yesterday. Do you think I wanted to do that? I'd give you the roof but there's a man up there with his three wives and his dog... or was it three dogs and his wife... anyway we're full. Gave the last room to a foreigner. Tall, skinny guy he was... don't know what he was doing here during a census but there you have it."

"A young couple you say?" said the Captain. "Was the woman pregnant?"

"No. Why would you think that?"

"We're looking for a baby," said Daniel.

"Well I'm sure there's quite a few babies in Bethlehem. But I did hear something about one

27

being born recently."

"Oh yes?" said Zaccheus.

"Joseph, the man's name was. Word is, he's a royal, from King David's line!"

"That's them," the Captain slipped out.

"Well I could tell you where they are, only... I'm not sure I should, I mean... privacy and all."

The shepherds nodded quietly. Respectful, but disappointed.

Then Paulo said gently, "We've been invited."

The inn-keeper brightened up again. "Oh, well that's different; you should have said so. The house just to the north of the main road into the town from here. I heard they found room there."

"Thank you very much," said the Captain and handed him one of his silver coins.

"Well, thank *you* very much!"

The five started along the road into Bethlehem. Many of the houses in the town had their lights off, but the one the keeper had indicated was lit. They led the sheep down a little hill and settled them nearby. Zacchaeus knocked on the door.

Evie whispered to the Captain, "I thought Jesus was born in a stable."

"Common belief based on Western tradition, not necessarily history. This house has two rooms."

"So?"

"One of them is probably where the animals sleep."

The door was opened by a lady holding an oil lamp and some cloths. "Yes? Can I help you?"

Zacchaeus stepped forward and took off his head gear. "Excuse me, but... we're looking for a Baby who's just been born. We were told He was here by an angel sent from the Lord. Lying in a manger, wrapped in cloths..."

"Oh my," said the woman weakly. "Really? Sent by an angel?"

"You have to believe us," said Daniel.

"Oh I do. I do. Believe me, today's been full of surprises. One more can't hurt. Come this way. But quietly." She stepped outside and walked quietly around the side of her house.

The Captain and Evie's hearts were battering down the wall of their chests shooting out tingles and prickles all over their bodies as they followed the woman in anticipation. There was a warm light glowing from within another entrance. A cool breeze blew at their backs, as though they were being gently nudged towards it.

The woman peeped her head in, and they heard her mutter quietly, "Mary, there are some visitors..." After a pause, she turned to the group of shepherds again, smiled, and nodded to them.

Wow, thought the Captain. *Wonder Of Wonders.*

"So we just..." said Daniel.

The woman nodded again. "Go on in."

Zacchaeus was first over the threshold, then Daniel, then the Captain, Paulo, and lastly Evie.

Two people from within looked up at them. One was a man with thick brown hair and beard, and the other was a girl lying on the hay-covered floor, propped up on her elbows and staring into a stone trough filled with straw. A little Baby was nestled in the middle. Swaddled in cloths. Fast asleep.

Neither Evie nor the Captain could believe their eyes. A hot flush came up and flooded their faces. The Captain came shoulder to shoulder with Paulo, making sure he had a full view of the sleeping bundle. He put a hand on his shoulder and said, in what was just a fraction over a whisper, "That's Him. That's the Creator of time and space."

Paulo stared ahead at the tiny helpless Baby, speechless.

CHAPTER

COME ADORE ON BENDED KNEE

"Forgive us," said Zacchaeus softly, "but we've come to see the Baby. We were told by an angel of the Lord that He's the Saviour and that this is where we would find Him."

"He's in a manger and everything," said Daniel. "Just like the angel said."

The man and the girl glanced at each other with astonished smiles. Then the man nodded and said, "Then of course, you should come in. Come and see."

They sheepishly shuffled forward, fixing their eyes on the sleeping Baby.

"I'm Joseph," said the man. "And this is Mary."

"Are you sure it's okay?" asked Daniel timidly.

"It's a *blessing* you're here," Mary nodded with a smile. It was a tired smile, but it came from her eyes with earnest. As though those eyes were a clear window to the soft, glowing heart within her.

"The angel told us that He is Christ the Lord," said Zacchaeus. "But how can this be so? Is a child going to deliver us from the Romans?"

"It's true," Mary replied. "An angel came to me as well and said that He'll be the Son of the Most High, and everything's happened the way it was said to me. Because..." her smile gleamed. "Well, nothing is impossible with God."

While they were talking, the Captain had been silently inching forward. The flickering flame of the oil lamps shone in the glossy sheen of his eyes. The swell of awe was blurring his vision. When he was still a few steps away and saw the face of the Baby, he lowered himself down. The straw covering the floor crunched under his knees; his eyes fixed on the Bundle in the trough.

The shepherds then also knelt. Evelyn was among them, but Paulo knelt down just so that he wasn't the only one standing.

Evie couldn't help feeling surprised when she looked at Mary. She didn't look much older than herself. She could quite easily have been one of her friends from school. And the Baby... He was a normal, average-looking baby. No halos, no glowing skin, just red and splotchy and wrinkled and smooshed up. He had thin strands of dark hair on His tiny head and milk spots on His baby-button nose.

"Who's this?" Mary said gently, having just noticed the girl with the shepherds.

Evie looked up. Their eyes met.

"What are you doing among these shepherds?" Mary asked softly and curiously.

Zacchaeus replied, "She was lost, and these two shepherds were helping her find her way home."

When Mary looked at Evelyn, she saw a face that could easily have been one of her friends back in Nazareth. They smiled at each other.

It was weird not seeing a halo or at least some sort of glow of light behind Mary's head. This girl in front of her was just... real. And although it relaxed Evie a little, her heart was still throbbing. "I'm... Evelyn. You must be such a... blessed woman or... however the phrase goes."

Mary smiled, blinked tiredly and gazed at her precious bundle in the manger. "I am feeling *so* blessed. Why He called *me* 'favoured one' and chose *me* to be Jesus' mother, I still wonder. I hope I can do a good job."

"Jesus. Is that His name?" said Zacchaeus.

Mary and Joseph nodded. "It's what the angel said to call Him," said Mary.

Evie shuffled forward on her knees to get a closer look. "I can't believe it's *Him*. He's so tiny."

"Would you like to hold Him?" said Mary.

All the blood left Evie's face. "What?"

"You can if you like."

Evie's insides squirmed and buzzed wildly. "But... He'll wake up, won't He? I don't want to disturb His sleep."

"He'll need feeding soon anyway. Here," Mary gently scooped up Jesus – His little legs stretching out and His throat making little baby grunting noises.

Evie glanced at the Captain with a worried, questioning look. For all she knew it might have ripped a hole in the fabric of time and space if she touched this Baby. But the Captain just smiled back at her and gave a tiny shrug and a nod.

Evie looked back at Mary who was holding Jesus in front of her, leaning in close. So, she prepared her arms to make the shape of a cradle, and the precious, warm little bundle was placed there. Evie lost her breath for a moment, and her eyes suddenly swelled with tears, which took her by surprise. As she looked down upon Jesus, His tiny eyes blinked open.

Does He know me? Does this Baby have powers to see into my soul? Is this meant to be happening?

She made sure to properly support His head and thought, *how can God be so dependent on my arms right now?* Instinctively, she placed a finger in His palm, and like a newborn baby will always do, He squeezed His tiny fingers around it.

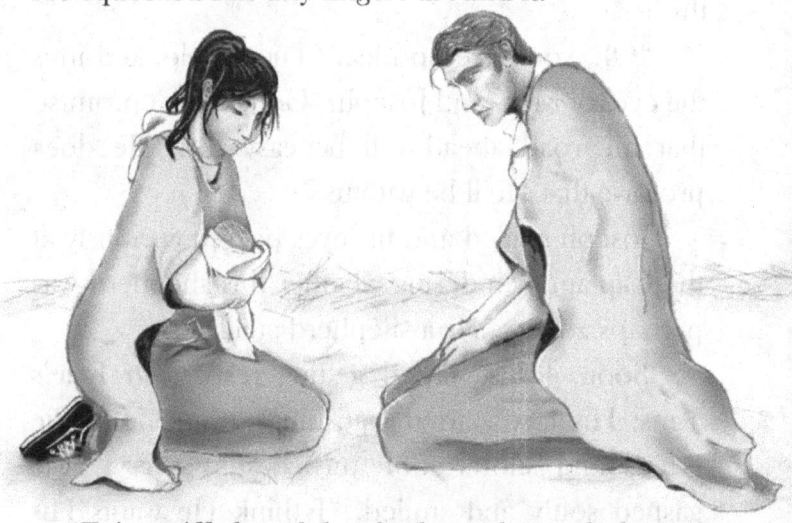

Evie sniffed and laughed gently, and then a small tear escaped and dropped down onto the Baby's cheek.

As she looked at her own tear on Jesus' face, she heard words in her head. Words she'd heard in church the other week, and it was as though the sound from Pastor Luke's lips then, was only now just reaching her ears.

He carried our sorrows.

The Captain was kneeling opposite her, muttering away softly, trying to take everything in. "How can we hold in our arms the King of kings? The Creator of all the universe contained in this... tiny body... It truly is a miracle."

"You know well," said Joseph softly, "...Who this is."

"Oh, you have no idea." Then he looked into the eyes of Mary and Joseph. "God doesn't promise that the road ahead will be easy. But He does promise that He'll be with us."

Joseph smiled and his eyes peered curiously at the Captain, wondering whether this shepherd was perhaps... not really a shepherd at all.

Soon, Jesus started getting restless in Evie's arms; His face started squishing up and His little grunts and snorts soon turned into a cry. Evie gasped softly and smiled. "I think He wants His mummy."

Mary smiled warmly as she received him back and nursed him.

Evie felt weak and fuzzy as she was left kneeling there, staring back at the Captain.

Morning was breaking and the small group of shepherds had been able to get two hours sleep in a nearby field before the sun was up. Zacchaeus' voice counting all the sheep was the last thing Evie remembered of that night.

As she woke, Evelyn needed the Captain to verify that she hadn't just dreamt it all. "Where will they go now?" Evie asked.

"Well, according to Matthew's gospel, they go to Egypt, obeying what an angel tells them to do in a dream."

"What do you speak of?" Zacchaeus said.

"Oh... nothing," said Evie. "What are *we* going to do now, Captain?"

The Captain was about to reply but Daniel said excitedly, "We're going to tell our friends what's happened. I can't wait. I'm going to tell everyone I meet!"

"So will you, I hope," said Zacchaeus to Paulo and the Captain.

"Believe me, I'm always trying," replied the Captain. They soon bid farewell to Zacchaeus and Daniel, and then travelled back to where the Train had landed.

"It shouldn't be far away now," the Captain said after they had been walking for a while. "Maybe I can get some of the controls working now that they've had a chance to think about their actions." He put on his piloting goggles that allowed his eyes to see the Train. "Well, it should be around here somewhere..."

"Maybe it's still a bit further," said Evie.

"No," replied the Captain, suddenly staring at some flattened grass at his feet. Flattened grass in the shape of train wheels. "It's been moved."

The others looked at what the Captain was looking at. The train once stood there, but as they could walk freely over the area, they knew without a doubt, that it was not there now.

CHAPTER

THE FAMILIAR STRANGER

"I'm sorry," Evie said. "I would normally be concerned about the Train being missing, but I just held baby Jesus and witnessed the first Christmas so there is no surprise that could top that at the moment."

"May I remind you that the Train is your only transport home," said the Captain.

"Yeah yeah. Hey, Captain... when I was holding Him..."

"Where could the Train have gone?" Paulo unintentionally interrupted.

"Well it'll be around here somewhere. We're not *without* it, we've just... *misplaced* it."

"How do you know? And how do you misplace

something that's invisible?"

The Captain thought for a second. "Actually, it's very easy to misplace something that's invisible."

"You know what I mean."

"Yes I do, and I don't have the answer yet but in order to find it, we'll need..."

"A special space-agey compass?" said Evie.

"Some sort of Train detector?" said Paulo.

"A change of clothes," said the Captain. He started walking back the way they'd come. "Come along."

"Where are we going?" asked Evie.

"To Bethlehem. Since Zacchaeus and Daniel took back their spare clothes, once again we look rather conspicuous."

"But that's ages away!" cried Evie.

"The walk will do us good."

"But we were just *there!*"

"Of course, we could always use this," said the Captain, holding up a gadget with knobs and dials and lights on it. "My Atom Relocating Molecular Teleport Device."

"You're kidding," said Evie flatly.

"But I only use it for emergencies."

Evie and Paulo were jogging to try and keep up again. "You can teleport?"

"Only once every twenty-four hours. That's why

it's for emergencies. I used it on the satellite."

"So *that's* how you popped up from nowhere," said Evie.

"But why every twenty-four hours?" asked Paulo, who was always interested in clever technology.

"That's how long it takes to recharge. Of course, if I was a fifty-first century Elite Sciren Official from the planet Kaponk, I'd have a better one. But I'm just me."

"You know," said Evie, "every time we ask you a question, you only go and open your mouth and create more questions."

"Sorry, I didn't realise. That's not on purpose."

When they had reached the outskirts of Bethlehem again, the morning sun had warmed them considerably.

"Can we see if that inn's got a vacancy now?" said Evie, leaning her hands on her knees and panting loudly. "My feet are killing me. I don't think I've walked so far in my life."

"How are you holding up, Paulo?" asked the Captain, his gaze fixed on the small town ahead.

"Fine," Paulo replied.

"Yeah alright, you don't have to rub it in. I'm unfit and I don't like P.E. at school. My teacher's nuts." Evie rested her hands on her hips and looked ahead. "So what do we do now that we're here?"

"Look for something out of the ordinary I suppose," said Paulo.

"Yes, but first," said the Captain, "you need a little knowledge of this time. In 4 B.C. there wasn't a lot of high-tech equipment. Just *equipment* would be a better description. To be able to move the Train, there would have to be something out of the ordinary somewhere."

"Let's hope it's in Bethlehem," puffed Evie.

"Well it's a good start." The Captain invited his passengers to go ahead of him into the town, while he followed closely behind enjoying their reactions to everything.

Evie and Paulo could hardly find the opportunity to blink their eyes. The busy street looked like a bustling community market. To Paulo's right, there was a man selling bread and to his left, there was a woman choosing between two live chickens. Then the smell of fish suddenly filled his nose.

"Fresh fish! Straight out of the Dead Sea! Top quality! You won't find any that's better!"

When Paulo realised he was talking to *him*, he had to politely decline.

Evie had seen a group of giggling kids running away from a crinkled old woman with a stick.

"Fresh herbs and root vegetables!" She twirled around to see a stall bursting with colourful produce.

"How much for this one?" she heard a woman say nearby, holding a garment in her hands.

"Only one bekah each," came a reply.

Evie called to the others. "Hey, you can buy clothes here. Is a... *bekah* expensive?"

"Quite reasonable," said the Captain as he and Paulo joined her. They started looking through all the handmade garments. There were robes, shirts, tunics and head scarfs made of different fabrics in all kinds of different colours.

"What's a bekah?" Evie whispered to the Captain.

"Half a shekel."

"What's a shekel?"

"Can I help you?" the seller asked them.

The Captain felt the fabric of the garments between his fingers. "Well?" he said, looking to Evie and Paulo. "Which ones do you like best?" Then he addressed the woman. "Are all the robes the same price?"

"The big robes... two bekahs each," she replied.

"Alright, I'll take three."

"Certainly. That will be one and a half shekels."

The Captain looked at some pieces of silver in

his hand. "Make it two?"

"Two shekels?"

"Alright, alright, make it a nice round five. Could you do them for five?"

"But sir, it is *I* who am selling them to *you*."

"How about six?"

Paulo whispered to Evie, "What's he doing?"

"He's haggling... but he's doing it the wrong way round. You're supposed to try and push the price *down*, not up."

"I'll take seven if you want me to, sir."

"Tell you what, seven is a bit of a funny odd number. It would make me happy if it was just a round ten."

"I cannot take that from you sir."

"Oh please. Go on. Surely you can stretch to ten shekels."

"...Well, if you insist."

"Splendid!" He gave the woman the shekels.

"How much money have you *got*?" Evie said as they were walking away.

"Oh, I'm a... bit of a collector," he replied.

The travellers put on their new robes which covered up most of the ordinary clothes.

"Now at least we look the part," said the Captain.

"Excuse me," said a voice nearby. They found

a young woman walking towards them, looking right at the Captain.

"Me?" said the Captain.

"I think so," she replied timidly. "Are you called the Captain? And are these not your friends Paulo and Evelyn?"

The Captain glanced at his companions with a curious frown. Evelyn was scared to answer in case it was some kind of trap. She suspected the Captain felt the same way but while they were thinking, Paulo blurted out, "Yes, that's us."*

"How do you know who we are?" asked Evie.

The Captain's eyes rolled. *So much for rule three.*

"Forgive me," the woman said, "but my brother described you to me, and you do rather stand out."

"What? Even with these new threads on?" said the Captain.

The woman looked down at their feet. "I've never seen such manner of footwear. I knew it had to be you."

"Who is your brother?"

"The shepherd, Zacchaeus. He came to the house early this morning and told me about what you had seen in the manger. He also told me that if

---

* Of all three of them, Paulo was the most trusting because his home planet consisted of very kind, peaceful and honest people.

45

I saw you in the market, I must make myself known to you. Offer you my home for food and rest."

A broad smile spread across the Captain's face. "Did he really?"

"He didn't seem to think that you were familiar with Bethlehem."

"And he was right. We do need a host to show us around," he said happily. "What is the name of our kind host?"

She placed a hand on her chest, "I'm called Rachel. Please, come to the house. I've just baked some bread."

"Sounds marvellous," replied the Captain, before turning around to his companions and adding, "I knew that young Zac was a good bloke!"

"Please, make yourselves at home." Rachel's house was a few streets away from the hustle and bustle of the markets, and surprisingly cool inside. They walked upon a floor of baked clay tiles, the walls were made of stone, and the thatch ceiling was only a few inches higher than the Captain's head. Shelves were cluttered with pots, bowls, spices and dried herbs, and there was a simple wooden table with a bowl that Rachel now filled with fresh fruit and vegetables from the market.

"Sit down and relax," Rachel said. "I'll pour some water. And help yourself to anything!"

The Captain, Evie and Paulo saw in one corner a large rug laid out with a few cushions placed about.

The Captain walked straight to the cushions and sat on the rug. "Ahh, luxury."

An older man then came in through the door, patting his large belly. "Ah, Rachel, you're back! I hope you have something for my hunger."

"Almost, father. You'll have to wait."

They hugged and kissed each other on the cheek before Rachel introduced the visitors to her father Elisha. Then she called out, "Mother, Miriam, Jared! Come and meet our guests."

Soon enough, in came an older woman with greying hair and hunched shoulders from an inner door which looked like it led to an outside courtyard. She had two young children with her – a boy of about seven and a girl of about four.

"This is my mother and two of my children Jared and Miriam. Mother, where is Daniel?"

"Asleep. Surely you don't want me to wake him."

"No of course not." Rachel addressed the visitors. "Daniel is my youngest boy. Six months old and the most beautiful baby you'll ever see."

"What about us?" said Jared.

"Well, *one* of the most beautiful babies," she said, tussling her son's hair and then tickling them both. "I named Daniel after..."

"Zacchaeus' friend?" Evie guessed.

"No, after the great prophet who survived being sentenced to the den of lions."

"Oh *that* Daniel," said Evie. She'd learnt about the prophet way back in Sunday School and how he was thrown into a pit of hungry lions for praying, but an angel came and protected Daniel in the lion's den... Then she got the song stuck in her head.

"And now the times are exciting," Rachel went on. "Zacchaeus said that the Saviour has come. The One who will deliver us from the Romans."

"I wouldn't hold your breath on that one," mumbled the Captain.

"Here is my famous herb bread with a hint of lemon," said Rachel, placing down on the table a large ceramic plate holding several slices of a golden loaf still steaming from the oven. "I'll finish preparing the rest of the breakfast."

The Captain stood up suddenly, "We don't have to stay for breakfast as well."

"I insist!" said Rachel, and that was that.

Breakfast was a smorgasbord of the barley bread, figs, dates, walnuts, pistachios and steamed fish. Evelyn had never felt so healthy. While they were eating, the Captain mentioned that he was looking for something, and it soon became apparent that it was something more than sheep. They were all eager to help and asked him what it was. "Well it's kind of a..." he began, "It's made of... and it's like a... well it's also sort of my mode of transport."

"A horse?"

"A wagon?"

"A mule?"

"No, it's... none of those things..." he said awkwardly. "But I suppose it's a little like a wagon."

"It's kind of hard to describe," said Evie, chewing on a pistachio nut.

"Very difficult," muttered Paulo. "It's even hard to *see* it, let alone describe it."

The Captain decided to try something else. "Has anything strange happened recently around these parts? A person, or a strange noise, a *feeling* even that... something was different? Not right?"

A room of blank faces stared back at him.

"Nothing that I can think of," said Rachel. "How about you, father?"

"Well, tax has stayed the same over the last few months," Elisha said. "*That's* strange. Usually it goes up. But I gather that's not the kind of thing you had in mind."

The Captain sighed quietly. How could he ask for help from people who hadn't even seen a train, let alone an invisible, time-and-space-travelling one? But despite their current mystery, the travellers lost track of time in Rachel's house; it was a joy to be there. They all met baby Daniel and had turns holding him. Evie played hide-and-seek with Jared and Miriam and chased them around the house. Eventually, Rachel's husband Noam came home from work and before they knew it, the sun was down and the house was lit with oil lamps.

They had lived a day as a family of ancient Bethlehem; sweeping courtyards, chopping vegetables, sharing in quiet devotions while a stew simmered, hearing the children's giggling running footsteps in between learning crafts and household chores, all beneath a roof that held the stories of three generations. It was during a quiet lull in their conversations after the stew that evening, that they all heard something that suddenly changed the happy mood. A distant scream.

Noam and the Captain jumped up and ran to the door. They heard the clopping of horses' hooves, and rickety wheels clattering over the roads.

"What is it Noam?" said Rachel, standing up.

"I don't know. Sounds like chariots. Have we paid all our taxes this month?"

"We are in no debt."

Elisha then went outside and stood by the road to see if he could see anything. Noam joined him, and Evie joined the Captain at the door.

"Something's not right," Noam said.

51

The screams had quickly turned to anguished cries, creeping through the town like a fast-growing virus. Men shouting, women crying, horses whinnying. Then, amongst it all, babies squealing.

Something in Evie's mind clicked as she remembered another story she'd learnt about in Sunday School. "Captain..." she said weakly. "Why did Mary and Joseph have to flee to Egypt?"

His face said it all. Evie's horrible suspicions were right. "They had to escape."

Dread drained the blood from her face. "Escape... what?" Although she already knew what.

"King Herod's order," he said. "The *massacre of the innocents.*"

They heard another baby shrieking, a woman pleadingly crying, and then another scream.

Evie suddenly exploded into action. "Rachel! Where's Daniel?"

"He's asleep in the crib, why?"

"There are soldiers coming."

"But we have done nothing wrong..."

"They don't need an excuse to be cruel," said the Captain, coming back into the room.

"You have to hide Daniel!" Evie said.

"I will protect *all* of my children!"

"But they're after *Daniel!*"

"Why would they be after Daniel? He's a

baby."

"Exactly!"

"Evelyn," said the Captain quietly. "You can't change a fixed event in history."

"I'm not. I'm trying to save one baby."

"What are you talking about?" said Rachel.

Elisha came tearing back inside, his face white. "It's the Romans," he said, almost choking on his words. "They're killing the babies."

"What?" said Rachel.

"A new baby was born last night, and you know who He is," the Captain said to Rachel.

"The Saviour," she said staring back up at him.

"A new King, the prophets say," said Noam.

"And King Herod doesn't want some other king growing up and overthrowing his kingdom."

"But my son is not this king," said Rachel, becoming weak with horror. "They may rest assured that Daniel is not the child Herod is afraid of!"

"They won't settle for that," said the Captain.

Evie turned to Rachel desperately. "Quick, where can you hide him?"

Rachel picked up Daniel from the crib.

Noam said, "But there's been a census Rachel. If you hide with Daniel, they'll wonder where you are. They'll know we're being dishonest."

"What will we do?" pleaded Rachel, tears

welling up in her eyes.

"Give him to me," said Evie. "I'm not in the census. There might be a chance."

Rachel handed Daniel over without hesitating.

"Go into the courtyard," Rachel's mother said. "There's a big chest where we keep linen, but it's empty; the linen is still in the washing. Go, *go!*"

"Evelyn," said the Captain. Evie's eyes met his, but he had no words. She had to hurry. He let her leave the room with the little six-month-old bundle in her arms.

"They're coming," cried Paulo, and the remaining party scurried away from the door as two Roman soldiers barged through.

Evelyn pulled her second leg inside the chest and lowered herself so that she could close the top. The inky blackness closed in around her. She heard a tiny sound from the baby.

"Where are your children?" one of the soldiers demanded.

Rachel stepped forward timidly and Jared and Miriam ducked behind her legs.

The second soldier strode over to them and tore them away from her.

"Th-th-these are my children," Rachel tremored.

"You'll not lay a hand on them!" said Noam

through gritted teeth.

The soldier just pushed Noam aside violently. The children screamed.

Evelyn could hear the voices. Her blood was going nuts, racing around inside her body, making her skin prickle with sweat. Daniel was waking up, she could feel it.

"These children are too old," said one solider to the other. "Let's move on."

The other soldier waited, standing firm. "You're Noam, son of Joab the farmer, aren't you? It is known you have two sons."

Noam swallowed hard, "Two *children*, that is. A son, and a daughter."

"If you lie..." he placed his right hand on the handle of his sword, which was for now, tucked away in its sheath. "Search the house," he ordered the second soldier.

It was not working. Daniel was awake, the darkness all around put him on edge and he could not smell his mother. Despite Evie trying to make him feel safe and secure, his little distressed voice broke the silence.

The soldier had searched the main room and was now coming upon the courtyard. All was deadly silent. Everything was still... Except, for the sudden muffled crying of a baby. The searching soldier looked straight at the chest in the courtyard. Rachel rushed out and dived to her knees at his feet.

The soldier wasted no time in opening the chest and with an angry kind of strength, he grabbed Evelyn out and took the baby from her grasp.

"But... but she's just a little baby," Evie yelled. "She's done nothing wrong!"

Daniel was squalling like a wild animal, but the soldier went still and narrowed his eyes. "A girl?"

Evie nodded quickly and swallowed. "What do you want with her?"

"Hurry up!" the first soldier called from the front room. "Let's keep it moving."

"This child tried to hide a baby girl."

"Forget the baby! Bring the child!"

The soldier gave the baby to Noam, who was standing beside Rachel and staring wide-eyed at Evie.

Then the soldier too looked at Evie with a piercing glare. "You have shown contempt and resistance against the decree of your ruler, King Herod. For this, you will be punished."

Evie looked straight at the Captain who was now in the doorway to the courtyard. He was trying to do some quick thinking – as Evie had just done.

"Bring her!" bellowed the first soldier, and then as Evie was grabbed by the arm and dragged through the house, everyone was saying something at once.

The Captain said, "You can't take her."

Noam said, "Take me instead. It's my fault!"

Elisha said, "Have mercy, she's just a child!"

Paulo said, "How can you punish someone for protecting a baby?"

Evie called out to the Captain, "Don't let them take me, Captain. Captain!"

Meanwhile, Rachel was still in the courtyard, blubbering with tears. Noam had handed Daniel down to her, and she cradled him and kissed his face over and over. At the same moment, Evie was being lifted up onto the back of a chariot.

The Captain yelled, "It's alright! We'll be right behind you!"

Within moments, the horses galloped away, and they were gone as quickly as they had come.

CHAPTER

CAPTURE

The Captain came running back inside the house. Noam met him in a huge embrace. "Captain! My son is alive because of Evie!"

"I need to get after her," he said urgently.

Elisha came up behind them both. "You will need transport. She could be in terrible trouble. Perhaps you could speak for her. Come."

Paulo was a speechless, motionless pillar in the middle of the room. Serothian history books looked nothing like this. The Captain had to prod him along so they could follow Elisha, who led them back through the house to the courtyard.

They soon came to the adjoining room that housed the animals. Elisha took the reins of two horses and brought them right through the house and out the front door.

The Captain smiled and took the reins.

"Now you'll have an excuse to come back and visit us," said Elisha.

"I didn't need an excuse," the Captain said, patting him on the back. "But we do need these horses. Thank you."

"May God go with you," he said and farewelled them both with kisses on the cheeks in traditional Jewish style.

"I must admit," said Paulo when they were leading the horses to the main road. "The people here are awfully nice. Just not the authorities."

"Ever ridden one of these?"

"Ah... no."

"...Right, we don't have much time, so you'll have to learn fast."

Evie felt like all her insides had been shaken up like the contents of a high-speed blender from the bumpy ride in the Romans' chariot. The path had been the worst dirt road you could imagine, and suspension was obviously not a thing yet. She didn't even have the luxury of being able to hold on properly, for her wrists were tangled up in ropes.

My butt's never felt so sore.

You're still alive though.

I'm holding onto that one positive point. I've only known the Captain a couple of days and I've already nearly died multiple times.

It's amazing you *are* still alive.

There's another chariot up ahead of us.

No other passengers though. Just you.

Obviously, everybody here learned long ago not to mess with these Romans.

The soldiers wore leather chest armour with a rich-red cape draping down the back, plated layers of leather on their shoulders, and studded strips making up a skirt that reached to the knees. They wore helmets of bronze with a metal piece on either side covering the sides of the face, and a bright red tuft like a broom-head made of horse's hair running from the

front to the back.*

They started speaking and Evie made sure to listen. She didn't have the headspace yet to try and figure out why they were speaking English.

"That last family," said the soldier who'd been bossing the other one around. "Didn't I say there were two sons? You went to look for the second."

"It was a daughter. You were mistaken."

"I see." There was a pause before he spoke again. Evie could almost hear the furrowing creases in his face. "This may be a silly question, but you did actually check it was really a girl?"

"Well... I didn't, no. I was about to. You called out that we had to go. I took them at their word."

"What? This brat could have lied!" He scowled down at Evie, who just stared dumbly back.

"They couldn't have known we were only after boys... should we go back?"

The first soldier paused again. "We go on. We got all the baby boys below the age of two. That's what we'll say. It'll be fine. No kings are going to come from that forgotten town."

Evie breathed deeply in relief and let it out slowly and silently.

---

* This brush-like feature on the helmet was called a 'crista', which means 'crest'.

After an hour of constant bumps and clatters and flying sprays of dust in the face, the wheels of the chariot finally stopped. Evie was tugged off the end of the chariot and, before she had a chance to stand up, they were dragging her towards the giant, black, eerie shape of a building. She struggled and thrashed her legs to try and get on her feet, kicking up clouds of dust in the process. Her new robe *was* going to make a great souvenir. Now it was ruined.

They came to a big opening in the building's outer wall, into a vast, sheltered courtyard. In through another smaller doorway was finally some light coming from flaming torches perched on the walls. She wished she could see ahead, but she'd run out of strength to be able to roll herself over.

"We wish to approach the king," said one of the soldiers. "We have returned from our assignment."

"Go in," said another voice.

In the brief break, Evie was finally able to stand up and have a good look around. They entered a large rectangular hall with fat pillars of stone spaced evenly about. There were deep red and purple drapes bunched and held together with gold tassels and jewels. It was all very nice, but it was who else was in the room that worried her. A large, aging man had emerged from behind some of the drapes and was making his way to a throne at one end of the

62

hall. He had a thick groomed beard, and was dressed in white robes with red trimmings, gold necklaces and chunky rings.

It's King Herod, Evie thought. Up until now, he'd just been a character in a story. Not a real person. But there he was. In the flesh. Large as life. Larger than the average human being anyway. He had eyes like cold, hard oak and when they shifted onto Evie, her stomach jumped up into her mouth.

King Herod was the villain right? In all the stories...

Oh, you remember your Primary School Christian-Ed lessons?

Maybe I should give him the benefit of the doubt. Maybe he was misunderstood...

Although, he did just order all the baby boys in Bethlehem to be killed... Just saying.

"Who is this reckless girl you bring to me?" Herod sighed, as he plonked himself onto his throne. His voice was smooth, but throaty and glutinous, as though he was trying to speak and swallow at the same time.

"A Bethlehem girl," replied one of the soldiers. "A rebel, opposing our authority. Since it was *your* decree and not Rome's, what would you have us do with her?"

Herod inclined his head to one side as he looked at her. Evie shifted uncomfortably. She wanted to run away.

"She is a mess. A tangled mess of a thing, but... I'm glad you kept her alive. She may have some use."

Evie couldn't stop herself. She burst out, "But I can't stay here. All I did was try to save my friend's little innocent baby! *None* of those babies are the new king you're looking for!"

King Herod leaned forward on his throne with an angry, suspicious glare. "What do you know of this *new king*?" One of his dark eyes was just a slit, and the other one was wide and shining with malice, peering at her.

Evie froze, then looked down at the floor. "Nothing. I don't know anything. Just... heard stuff."

Herod held his stare for what felt like a whole minute. Then he sat back and growled, "Aah, take her away, I don't wish her to be my problem. You," he said to one of the soldiers. "Take her to your home and make her one of your slaves if you wish."

Evie looked up, "But..."

"And teach her how to speak to a king."

The soldiers bowed their heads, turned around and marched out of the palace. Evie was not ready for their brisk departure and so she stumbled to the ground again. The one Herod spoke to was the one who had opened the chest's lid in Rachel's house. When they came outside, he took Evie's ropes in his hands. The other soldier rode the chariot away.

She expected the soldier to say something, but he just started walking again, yanking on her rope. Her feet kicked up more dust as she continuously tripped over her robe. Her wrists were grazed and bruised.

I don't know if I can take much more of this.

CHAPTER

NEW HOME

|||||||||||||||||||||||||||||||||||||||||||||||||||||||||||

This must be Jerusalem, Evie thought. *I'm pretty sure King Herod lived in Jerusalem.*

What you want is a street sign.

Have they even been invented yet?

Street signs aren't high tech.

Anyway. It really doesn't matter where I am.

You're right. What matters is whether the *Captain* knows where you are.

Now that would be handy. Does he?

Sorry no. But he might work it out... eventually.

The soldier, Evie's new master, slowed down and arrived at a quiet village of stone houses not far beyond Herod's palace.

The night was thick. Bone still and dead dry.

Evie's throat was about to crumble up like sand and she suddenly realised how tired she was.

The soldier finally stopped at the door of one of the stone houses, which was opened to them.

"You're late," said the woman who'd opened the door. "And who's this?"

"We had to ask the king what to do with her. She disobeyed the law. From Bethlehem."

"Why bring her here?"

Why are they all speaking English? Evelyn thought again.

"He gave her to us."

"We already have a servant."

"Why do you question, Cassia? There are some who'd give an arm to have two servants."

"Never mind, I'll find use for her." The woman looked at Evie. "What is her name?"

"Evie," Evie butted in, tired of being talked about like she wasn't there. "*My* name's Evie."

"You are not required to speak," said the soldier beside her.

"You'd better bring her in, Lucius. Let's not have her standing out there in the night."

Evie felt a spark of hope in her heart. Maybe her employers weren't going to be cruel. *Are they called employers when they won't be paying me?*

she wondered. *Slaves don't get paid do they?*

The woman disappeared back into the house, and once the soldier, Lucius, had brought Evie into the first room, he faced her towards him, looked at her and inspected her clothes. He took the heavy, dusty fabric of the robe in his hands, gave it a shake and straightened it up a bit. In the process, the left shoulder of her jacket and part of her jeans were revealed. She looked up at him, biting her bottom lip. His face slowly frowned, then the woman called from another room.

"Bring her here, Lucius."

Lucius prodded Evie into a small area lighted only by an oil lamp the woman was holding. It made strange, flickering shadows that wriggled on the walls. Then Lucius left and the woman showed Evie two mats laid out on the floor. She threw a rug onto one of them. "This is where you shall sleep, Evie. You may sleep now. You're no use to us heavy-eyed."

"Um... thank you?" Evie said timidly.

"There is another slave, whose name is Felicia. She will show you how to do things tomorrow."

"Where is she?"

"She's not yet finished her duties."

Wow. What is it? 11pm?

68

Cassia started to leave.

"What do I call you?" Evie asked.

She turned around. "Mistress will do."

"I don't... I'm not... I mean, I've got friends who are looking for me. I don't belong here."

"You broke the law, so you will face whatever consequences your king decides."

"He's not... well... I was only trying to save a baby's life."

Cassia's eyebrows twitched downwards. It looked like she had questions, but she just said, "You cannot take it up with me. It is not my business."

"But I'm not even from around here."

"You are from Bethlehem. I know."

"No, I'm from another... well, I come from somewhere a long way away."

"Well, now this is your home. Go to sleep Evie. When you wake, you will be more cheerful."

I doubt it. Evie couldn't tell whether it was an encouragement or an order.

In the gloom of a downstairs room of another Roman household, Marius' wife called from the bed. He sluggishly obeyed, trudging up the narrow, winding steps.

"What on earth are you doing? Come back to bed and get some sleep, Marius."

"When are we expecting our visitors again?" Marius asked, slipping inside the covers.

"Lucius and Cassia are coming tomorrow."

"Why must they come? I'm a very busy man."

"Cassia is my sister. And I hardly ever see her anymore. I don't know why we had to stay in this house when we got married anyway."

"Because I built it myself and I cannot leave it."

"Yes I know. Because of whatever it is that you've got down in that underground room."

"It's important."

"Yes. So important, you don't even allow *me* to go down there." She said cynically, "I suppose it's a nice birthday surprise for me or something." When she got no reaction out of him, she just said, "I hope it's not something strange or dangerous... Marius? Are you listening?"

Marius snored.

CHAPTER

THE EMPTY BUSY ROAD

"Whoa, whoa, whoa! How do I stop this thing again?" Paulo asked urgently.

"Pull on the reins, my friend, and..."

Paulo pulled hard. The horse raised its front hooves off the ground, sending Paulo sliding off its back and into a heap on the dusty ground behind it.

"...and hold on," finished the Captain. He jumped off the side of his own horse. "Now I'll have to get you back *on* there again."

Paulo scrambled to his feet, dusting off his hands. "It was hard enough the first time."

"You're lucky Elisha didn't give us two camels."

"Can we afford a short break? I'm spent!"

"Certainly not!" the Captain said, holding out a

hand for Paulo. "We've had a hard day's night, but we can't stop now. Evelyn could be in trouble."

"I don't think I've ever felt tireder."

"*More* tired. You've never felt *more* tired. And I know, at this time of night, we should be sleeping like logs, but we must..."

"Must find Evelyn first. I know."

The Captain helped Paulo back onto the horse.

"Tireder *is* a word," Paulo said as they gently built up to a trot again.

"Maybe on Serothia."

The road they were on had brought them to a tall, wide-stretching city wall with a big gate that was patrolled by some Roman soldiers.

"Jerusalem," the Captain mumbled, staring up at the wall with an excited glint in his eye.

"What makes you think Evie's in this town?"

"Because this is not just a town, this is the capital of Judea... where punishment for crimes happen."

"I see. You think..."

"Well there's only one way to find out for sure," he said a little nervously.

"What's that?"

"Go to the palace. Where King Herod lives."

"And this is the king who just ordered his soldiers to kill all the baby boys in Bethlehem?"

"Yes."

Paulo swallowed. "How did the king know about Jesus anyway?"

"Apparently, a group of wise astronomers learned of the birth of a 'New King' by reading it in the stars. They wanted to pay their homage and asked King Herod where he was, thinking he'd know about it. So it was *them* who made Herod aware of it." He frowned and muttered, "Obviously that's all happened already."

"And you said Jesus went to this other place..."

"Egypt yes. They must be on their way now. Rest assured, no harm will come to Jesus." The Captain frowned to himself, "Not yet anyway."

Dawn was slowly creeping across Jerusalem. Evelyn yawned as she admired the beautiful sunrise.

"I would get out of that habit if I were you," Felicia scolded. "You might easily do it in front of the master and the gods help you then."

"What do you expect when I've had five hours sleep? I thought Cassia wanted me well rested."

"Mistress to you."

"Anyway, Lucius didn't seem such a bad guy to me. Besides having to carry out dodgy orders. And I can't help it if I have to yawn." Saying the word made another one come.

"Don't say I did not warn you."

The two girls were out the front of the house. Felicia was sweeping the stone path around the door and Evie was soaking some clothes in a big wooden bowl under Felicia's instructions.

"So how come Lucius isn't off to the palace, or whatever you call it, to work for King Herod this morning?"

"He's been given some leave. They're visiting the Mistress's sister today and staying a few days."

"What will we do while they're gone?" The word 'escape' filled Evie's mind.

"We won't be here. People take slaves with them when they go on trips. Although, they may only take one of us. And it'll probably be you."

"But you're more experienced."

"Yes but you're new. They're not going to trust you here by yourself."

How on earth is the Captain going to find me if I keep getting moved around? Evie thought uneasily, just as something *plinked* onto the ground next to Felicia's foot. "What's that?" Evie said.

"What?" Felicia frowned, even more grumpy from being interrupted from her work again. Evie wondered if she was born with that frown.

"*That*, that just fell out of your pocket thing."

Felicia looked down and went to grab it, but Evie beat her to it. It was a small round silver coin, about two centimetres in diameter.

"Never mind what it is," Felicia scowled.

"It's pretty." Evie was just about to give it back to her, but something caught her attention. Something was very wrong with it. She turned it over in her hand and her eyebrows shot upwards. "How'd you come to have this coin?"

"I found it," Felicia grunted, snatching it back and putting it deep into her pocket. "Just found it when I was working, that's all."

"Why're you being so cagey? I was just curious."

"Cagey?"

"Er... secretive."

Felicia came nearer and whispered in a harsh rasp, "Why do you *think*? We slaves have nothing. And that's the way it's supposed to be. If I am caught with this, it will be taken from me. And, as you say, it's pretty. It is probably worth nothing, but I want to keep it." Felicia returned to her duties.

"Where *exactly* did you find it?"

"I did not steal it if that's what you're thinking. Now get back to work, before the master finds us here just chatting."

Evie returned to her washing. But in her mind's eye, all she could see was that coin. Something was very wrong here, and she didn't need to be an expert time-traveller to know it. She didn't know what Augustus Caesar's face had looked like, (or any other king from anywhere for that matter).

But what she *did* know, was that they didn't have *shillings* in ancient Jerusalem. And what's more, the year stamp on it said *1934!*

Evie soon learned that Lucius and Cassia were indeed going to be taking her on their trip. She had to help Cassia pack her things and everything was placed on a wooden cart with two wheels at the back. Evie was relieved when she saw Lucius tying a weary looking mare to the front of the cart. For all she knew it was going to be *her* pulling that cart along. She'd never been so thankful in her life, for a horse.

When it was eventually time for her to climb up onto the cart, she glanced wistfully down the road, wishing that the Captain and Paulo would suddenly appear. She would jump down off the cart quicker than the Captain could say *Shooting star!* And run away from Lucius and Cassia and grumpy Felicia without a worry in the world.

But the road was completely Captain-and-Paulo-*less*. Which made it seem empty, even though it was bustling with people.

She ached all over. From the work, from the poor excuse for a bed, from her loneliness, and from the uncertainty of her fate. Even her mind ached. It would not stop thinking about that coin.

The Captain and Paulo, instead of conveniently roaming down Lucius and Cassia's street at that moment, were actually standing outside King Herod's palace. There were several Judean soldiers standing like matching sturdy trees at the entrance wearing leather chest armour and pointy bronze helmets.

The Captain waltzed right up to the nearest soldier and said. "Good day my good man. I'd like to see the king, please."

"You'd like to see the king?" said the soldier in a mocking, sarcastic voice. "King Herod?"

"Of course. Unless there's more than one? I know there were a lot of Herods but not at the same time."

"You can't just *speak to the king*, just like that. Are you being funny?"

"No," sniggered the other one. "Just dumb."

"I can speak perfectly well, thank you."

"I think they mean you're stupid, Captain," said Paulo.

"I beg your pardon Paulo? Tame your tongue!"

"Not *me*, *I* don't think you're stupid."

"Why can't we talk to the king?" the Captain asked the soldiers.

"He doesn't just speak with civilians on request. You have to wait until he holds court."

"Shooting star," he muttered, "when I want to speak to *my* King, I can do it any time of day or night."

"What's this about another king?"

"We're just searching for a girl," Paulo cut in. "We think she was brought here late last night..."

"That's right," said the Captain. "But she was brought by *Roman* soldiers. Her name's Evelyn..."

"Forget it. She'll be long gone."

"What do you mean?" said Paulo. "Have you seen her? Please, just tell us what happened to her. Where did she get taken? She's our friend."

"Young thing with black scraggly hair?" the soldier said with a discomforting sneer.

The Captain and Paulo's stomachs squirmed.

But then the soldier's smile dropped. "She was lucky. Usually, offenders like that go down to the dungeons. But the king didn't want her there. Said she'd be too troublesome or something like that."

The Captain pursed his lips into a private smile. Evelyn could certainly make a nuisance of herself when she set her mind to it.

"So she ended up as a slave," the soldier finished. "In one of the Roman quarters."

"Who? Where?"

"That's enough. The rest is the king's business."

They shrunk away, with more questions hanging on their lips than they started with. But at least they knew she was alive. And she would have a roof over her head for the time being. They would just have to find her.

10

THE CLOSED DOOR

It was the rattle and bumps of the wagon stopping that woke Evelyn. She had a vague sense that she'd just dreamt of home.

"We're here," said Cassia's voice beside her. "Get up and help me carry our things indoors."

Evie got up slowly, rubbing her eyes and stretching out her legs. A house stood before them, similar to Lucius and Cassia's own house. But it was bigger and there was a lot more open space around; they must have travelled to the outskirts of the city.

A woman emerged from the house, wearing a long red floaty robe with gold trimmings, which flapped against her silky olive skin. She held her arms out to greet them. "Cassia, it's good to see you!"

"I'll just get my bags from the cart," said Cassia.

"Let your servant do that!" the woman said. "Come in and have a drink."

And with that, Evie was left outside by herself. "Oh for goodness sake!" she said out loud when she was alone. "Yeah, just make *me* do *everything*." She trudged all the bags inside and asked drearily where they should go. Then she had to take off their shoes, prepare Lucius and Cassia's bed for the night, and unpack the rest of their belongings.

When she had a brief moment to herself, she couldn't resist a little snoop around to see what *this* house was like. She came to a closed door and wondered what was behind it. Without too much thought, she laid a hand on the door handle.

"What are you doing?"

Evie jumped with a gasp and turned around. A teenage boy stood there in a simple tunic and belt. He had a large nose, cushiony brown lips, dark shadows under his eyes and smooth, rich golden skin. His eyes were the colour of her Nanna's old mahogany sideboard, and they stared at her the way Nanna's did when Evie accidentally scratched it when she was eight. Nervously, Evie answered, "I was just er..."

"Sneaking around?"

"No. I wasn't."

"The master doesn't like servants sneaking about. Go back to your duties."

"What's through that door?" Evie asked before she could stop herself.

"That's none of our business. No one's allowed down there. Only the master, Marius. Now come away from there."

"Who are you?"

He sighed. "I'm Levi. Marius' servant."

"I'm Evie," she said as they started walking away from the closed door. "Is it just Marius and the lady who live here? Is she his wife?"

"Yes. Her name's Portia."

"Is she nice?"

"If you do as you're told."

Later that night, Evie lay wide awake, tossing and turning again. She had no idea what the time was. *If only I had my book to read,* she thought. The book she was reading at the moment was called *Mysteries of Space and The Fourth Dimension.* But then it occurred to her, *who needs to read up on theory when I'm right here living out the real deal?* She'd been fascinated by space and time travel ever since she saw her dad watching Tom Baker create a time loop in order to put the destruction of a spaceship on hold, in a re-run of the old *Doctor Who* series. She never dreamed that any of it could be real. And that it would happen to her!

Even though she was tired, her mind was buzzing. She couldn't switch it off. Soon, she realised she could hear someone moving about in the house. In the middle of the night. She lifted her head from the pillow to listen. It wasn't Levi. He was fast asleep on the other bedroll near her. It could easily have been any of the others, only, it sounded like someone coming *in* from the outside. When she heard the creak of a door opening, her body bolted upright. She pictured that closed door. The one 'only Marius' was allowed through...

She heard the footsteps gradually fade away. Her mind wasn't allowing her a wink of sleep anyway. She silently crept out of bed...

11

A LITTLE MIDNIGHT GARDENING

"You act like you know exactly where we're going," Paulo commented wearily as he and the Captain were walking through the streets of Jerusalem. The moon lay a ghostly veil over everything. The streets were dead.

"Do I?" replied the Captain. "Oh, that's good. That's the look I was going for."

"So, you *don't* know where we're going?"

"I didn't say that."

"So, you *do* have an idea?"

"I didn't say that either."

Paulo had the most tired expression on his face and his shoulders drooped in a silent sigh. "We've been chasing Roman soldiers all day, and nothing. Finding the right one could take weeks!"

"What?!" the Captain took off ahead, leaving Paulo with the two horses.

"Well it *could!*"

The Captain just waved his hand in Paulo's general direction, crouched down and looked at the ground.

Paulo joined him, peering down. "What is it?"

"This plant. Don't you think it looks a bit peculiar?"

Paulo knelt beside him. "Every plant around here looks peculiar to me. What's wrong with it? Is it not supposed to grow in this area?"

"It's not supposed to grow on this *planet.*"

"Really?"

"That is to say, not this world. It's from... somewhere else."

"What is it?" Paulo reached out to feel its strange velvety leaves.

The Captain slapped his hand away fiercely. "Don't touch it!"

"Ouch."

"Sorry about that, but it's deadly. Your finger didn't brush over the top of it did it?"

Paulo shook his head honestly. He had to settle for looking. Its tiny leaves were dark green with a smoky purple tinge, and it covered a small patch of ground like short woolly grass.

"It's not deadly if you just touch it," the Captain clarified. "But if you bit your nails or ate a sandwich or picked your nose or anything afterwards, you'd be a goner."

"What's it doing here?"

"That's what I'd like to know."

"I wonder if anyone's touched it."

"Precisely what I've been thinking."

"Could it be related to the Train being missing?"

"Yes, I've thought about that."

"It could be a lead."

"Yes, that's what I think."

"You do think about a lot of things at once."

"That's me. The Thinker. I was the one Auguste Rodin roped in to pose for his famous sculpture. It turned out looking a lot musclier than me though so I half suspect that he ditched his first attempt and got someone else to model. Rude."

Paulo didn't know what that meant,* so he just asked, "What do we do now?"

"Well we can't leave this here. We'll have to dig it up. Only, my gardening

---

* In case you also don't know, *The Thinker* is a very famous sculpture of a man sitting down thinking very hard about something.

gloves are on the Train. Drat."
The Captain went and sat down
on a tree stump, one arm
leaning on his knee and his
chin resting on the back of
his other hand. "Think, think,
thinkety think," he said to himself.
Then he stood up and walked
back over to the horses.

Hanging from the
saddle of the Captain's
horse was a hessian bag.
He tugged it off and handed it to Paulo. Then he
started digging up the plant with a couple of fallen
sticks. "We'll need to collect it up, roots and all, into
that bag."

Paulo was about to ask how, but he thought of
the Captain's fourth rule.♦ He remembered he was
wearing two sets of clothes. His own sky-blue
overalls, underneath his new Bethlehem robe. He
unwrapped himself from the robe and used the
material as gardening gloves.

The Captain looked up from his dusty job to
wipe away some sweat from his brow. "What are

♦ The Captain didn't believe in *stupid* questions, but his fourth rule was to
not ask too many *unnecessary* questions. With just a little thinking or
waiting, or doing or praying, answers usually revealed themselves.

you doing in your overalls?"

Paulo started scooping with the robe.

"Oh, good thinking," the Captain said.

"This stuff doesn't look very deadly," said Paulo after a short while.

"Never underestimate the Kratilier Lumis."

"The what?"

"That's its scientific name. It's more commonly known as the Violet Assassin. Assassin means killer."

Paulo swallowed. "Now I believe you."

Once finished, the two of them straightened up and stood back.

"Well," said the Captain wiping his brow again. "That's got it all I think."

"I don't think deadly plants exist on Serothia."

"In its native home, some animals use it to trick their prey into eating it. When it flowers it looks like a beautiful bright blue and yellow fruit you see. The victim eats the flower, they wander around a bit and then die. Easy lunch."

"Horrible."

"Fact of life. Only not for us if we accidentally touch this stick or your robe. We'd better burn these when we get the chance."

"Oh I'm... sorry about the robe."

"It's alright. Plenty more where they came

from." The Captain took the bag and attached it to the horse's saddle. "Let's see if there's any more of it growing around the place."

As the Captain and Paulo both turned, they froze in place. They couldn't get any further. Something, or rather some*one* was in their way.

"Paulo," said the Captain, out the corner of his mouth. "Is it just me, or is there a rather large intimidating Roman soldier with impressive muscular structure standing in front of us?"

"You're breaking the law," said the rather large, intimidating Roman soldier with impressive muscular structure in front of them.

"Oh, hello," the Captain said, looking up at him. "I'm the Captain and this is my friend Paulo. How do you do? Would you mind telling us what law we've broken, exactly?"

"You're trespassing on private land, and you're destroying precious vegetation."

"Well I'll give you the trespassing bit, but that was *not* precious vegetation. Not in these parts."

The soldier narrowed his eyes and took one giant step towards the hessian bag.

"Be careful. It's deadly," the Captain said.

The soldier opened the bag and went to plunge his hand inside, but Paulo shouted "No!" and quickly pulled the Roman's hand away.

The soldier's eyes stabbed Paulo's harshly. "You dare to touch me? Bruttius. Otto." He was not alone. Two other Roman soldiers approached, then the first one looked back at Paulo and the Captain. "You will be repaid for this."

The Captain smiled, modestly, "Oh thank you very much. But saving people from deadly things is just in a day's work for us."

"Arrest these men," the first soldier said to the other two. Bruttius and Otto came and grabbed them. Their strong arms were like steel bars.

Then Paulo and the Captain were pulled away from the scene. Meanwhile, the bag of Violet Assassin was left resting unattended against the horse's side.

CHAPTER

12

THE PRICE TO PAY FOR PRYING

Evie crept through the dark stillness of the house and soon arrived at the mysterious door. It was open. Still wafting closed behind whoever had just gone through. She quickly slid her body in through the small gap before it completely swung shut. It was pitch black apart from a small moving glow of light, disappearing around a corner, downwards. Evie quickly realised she was standing at the top of a long, winding passageway of steps, spiralling downwards, into the musty earth. She followed the torchlight silently, keeping her steps in time with the torch-bearer's steps.

Suddenly, the light was still, the footsteps stopped. Evie froze. She dared not even breathe. It felt like minutes, but of course it was only a few seconds. The footsteps started again, and the light proceeded deeper down.

About another fifteen steps further, the stairs finally opened out onto a dark room. Evie quickly retreated back up a few steps to hide herself, while she listened to the sounds that came from the room. There was a grunty sigh, and then a sound that should not have been around for another two thousand years or so. The sound of some kind of machine or computer booting up. Evie wanted so much to use her eyes as well as her ears. She leaned forward slightly, poking her head a little way out into the open. There was still quite a lot of wall in the way, so she went back down one more step and leaned around a fraction more.

She saw the figure, luckily facing away from her. Whoever it was wore a long black cloak with a hood over the head. The torch had been hooked up on a fixture on the wall – a sconce, and in front of the person, in the middle of the floor, stood a strange object. It was about the size of a suitcase, sitting on top of a small wooden table, and a subtle glow of light was coming from somewhere inside it. At the top was a hole of blank space bordered by messy wires and some crudely put-together pipes of some kind, all pointing inwards to the empty space. The shilling popped into Evie's thoughts again. Here was something else that clearly did not belong in 4 B.C.

The hooded figure fiddled with some of the parts on the humming object and Evie started to notice a vague image working its way into midair between the wires and pipes. Before long, her eyes widened as she began to recognise what it was an image of. Although she couldn't quite see it all, it looked very much like a steam train, blurring into view. She had seen the Captain's Train once before, with his special glasses. She was not wearing those glasses now, and yet she could see its image. She leaned out a tiny fraction more to try and get a better angle, but she couldn't... quite... see... whether...

Her bare foot slipped off the step. It made a quiet *slap* sound against the hard, stone floor. It may as well have been a clap of thunder. She froze and looked up. The hooded head snapped around. She turned and darted up the steps, two at a time. In the next second of course, there were running footsteps after her.

The stairway quickly darkened. Her foot missed a step and she fell forward, landing painfully on her stomach. Her voice yelped an involuntary cry. Before she could scramble back to her feet, a large hand clutched her ankle. She kicked and yanked to get herself free, but its grip was too strong.

She felt herself being pulled back down the steps. As she tried to gather all her strength to break free again, another hand grabbed her around the waist and then the hand that had yanked at her ankle was now clasped around her arm and she was hauled up off the ground and back onto her feet.

She could sense it was a man. He pulled her in tightly in front of him so that she could no longer use her arms. He shoved her back down the steps, while she kicked and protested with her legs. She tried to get a grip on the steps with her feet but he only lifted her up higher and carried her to the bottom like she was a paper plate.

When he reached the bottom, he dropped her onto the hard floor and then headed straight to the machine to turn it off. He leaned over her, a cowering, quivering dry leaf on the floor. He was a middle-aged man with a thick beard, Roman clothes under the black cloak, and a gruff, angry face. He stabbed some words at her. "Who are you?"

"I'm Evie."

"Who?!"

"C-C-Cassia and Lucius' s-slave."

He sighed gruffly. "The in-laws."

"Y-you must be M-Marius."

With an angry, raspy whisper, he demanded, "What are you up to? What do you know about this place?"

Evie stuttered. "N-n-nothing, honestly. I don't know anything."

"You lie!"

"I don't lie. I have no idea what all this is!"

He pushed his hand harshly over her mouth and glanced up the passageway. "You make too much noise."

Evie looked up at him, trembling. The torch light was flashing in his huge, moist, black pupils.

"Tell me the truth," he whispered angrily. "Why did you follow me down here? You have no business here." He uncovered her mouth.

She whimpered, "I... heard a noise. That's all."

"Did it occur to you that you were sticking your nose where it does not belong?!"

She nodded, then quickly shook her head. She didn't know what to say.

"What have you seen?"

"Nothing. Nothing!"

He looked at her distrustfully. Then he pulled at her dusty robe. "Stand up."

She stood, and then wiped her runny nose with the back of her hand.

He said terrifyingly softly, "You will forget everything you have seen here, and you will not come down here again, understand?"

Without hesitating, Evie nodded with passion. But inside, she knew she couldn't just forget. This man knew something about the Train and so really, this was just the beginning.

"We're going back up to the house now," Marius said. "You will not speak of or even think any more of this... or I will have to get rid of you."

He didn't have to explain what 'get rid of you' meant. She nodded and they walked up the steps together, in silence.

A raucous, insistent rooster squawked noisily somewhere and woke the Captain and Paulo from their terrible sleep. The Captain sat himself up and clutched his back, "Urgh!" Paulo lifted his head and clutched his neck, "Ow!"

"You look almost as bad as I feel," said the Captain looking at Paulo as the early morning light trickled down through the slats in the ceiling into the damp, smelly, stone room. "Still, I've had worse sleeping arrangements."

"You've slept in worse than a... what did you call this place?"

"A dungeon."

Paulo eyed a pile of bones in the corner with

unease.

"Well at least we're in out of the weather," said the Captain cheerfully.

"How long will we be here do you think?"

"They said they'd come for us first thing."

"And what if our punishment's worse than this?"

"For digging up a bit of garden? I hardly think..."

"No, for me supposedly assaulting a soldier."

"Oh. Yes. I keep forgetting about that bit. Not to worry. Just let me do the talking."

They heard the rattling of keys and looked up. Paulo jumped with fright as the pile of bones in the corner also stirred. It turned out there was still some living skin left on it.

"Oh, good morning," said the Captain to the bones. "Sorry if we woke you."

There was movement from an entrance on their level and a Roman soldier came in and released the two travellers. It was the one called Bruttius from last night, and soon, as they were escorted out of the dungeon, they rejoined with Otto and the other solider whom they had first met.

They came to an open, airy patio with fine curtains which floated on the fresh, morning breeze. There was a brass desk in the middle and it appeared as though they were waiting for somebody to come and sit down at it. In the meantime, the Captain said, "I suppose it's too much to hope that there might be a cup of tea coming, Bruttius?"

There was no response.

"Otto?"

Again, no answer.

"What's *your* name by the way?" he asked the other soldier.

"Silius," he said, staring straight ahead.

The Captain looked back at him as if he didn't believe the man. Then he glanced at Paulo and both of them shared a small, silent chuckle.

Then another soldier came in and, as predicted, he sat down at the desk. The three Roman soldiers removed their bronze helmets and held them under their arms.

"Do you have anyone to represent you in trial?" the seated soldier asked them.

"No," replied the Captain, "but it can be arranged if you give me a day or two."

"Very well, the trial will now commence. Will you present the crimes com..."

"Wait, wait, wait, hold on!" objected the Captain, "I don't have anyone to represent me, I just said that."

"The trial must take place at the present time.

What crimes have these men committed?"

Silius answered, "They were both partaking in the destruction of the king's property."

"Digging up the ground," clarified Bruttius.

"Do you have any reasoning for your actions?" the one at the desk asked Paulo and the Captain.

The Captain opened his mouth to speak, but Paulo answered. "Yes. We were digging up a dangerous plant so that it couldn't harm anyone."

"There is no dangerous vegetation in Jerusalem," said the man behind the desk. "This deed will not bring about major punishment. Perhaps they were mistaken about the plant. I will give them a small fine."

"That is not all," said Silius.

Paulo's eyes drooped shut.

"The younger one attacked me."

"Attacked?" scoffed the Captain in Paulo's defence. "It was hardly an attack."

"Silence," said the seated soldier. "How did he attack you?"

"He forcedly twisted my arm when I reached into one of their horses' saddle bags."

"That's because the deadly plant was *in* that bag," said Paulo. "If you'd have touched it, you'd have been in a lot of trouble!"

"You have stated that no one is here to

represent you, and so you shall remain silent."

"Hang about," said the Captain. "In that case, *I'll* represent him."

"And what have *you* to say?"

"Well... the deadly plant was in that bag and if he'd have touched it, he'd have been in a lot of trouble." He looked at Silius. "You could be dead by now!"

"The man is making a threat," said Silius.

"No I'm not."

"Did you intend to harm this soldier?" the man at the desk asked Paulo.

"No. I intended to save his life."

"I do not believe what you say about the deadly plant. But because no lasting harm has been done, I will merely issue you a fine."

"Fair enough," said the Captain. "You've been very reasonable. How much?"

"Three hundred denarii."

"Three hundred denarii, now let me see, I have two coins in this pocket and... one, two, three... three... THREE HUNDRED DENARII!!?"

"You protest?"

"Isn't that... nearly a year's wage? I can't pay that much."

"You oppose the law?"

"What I mean to say is that... I don't *own* that

much. Neither of us do. If we did, we'd be more than happy to give it to you..."

"But you are wealthy, you have fine clothes and even a ring on your finger." He noticed a simple silver band around the Captain's pinky.

"Yes but, that's *why* I don't have money, because I just spent it all buying these clothes."

"Your ring may suffice. What is its weight?"

The Captain looked up at him. "I can't give you this ring."

"Unable to, or won't?"

"I won't. It... it was my grandfather's."

"So be it," said the man, becoming impatient. "You have made this choice." He stood up and said one word that Paulo didn't like the sound of at all. "Banishment."

13

THE DEAL

"What does one do when one's been banished, Captain?" said Paulo.

"I don't know exactly. We live, well... we survive. I'm no expert on being banished, it's only ever happened to me once before. But that time I... kind of deserved it."

The hot sun pressed down on their tired, aching bodies. The earth beneath their feet was dry and mountainous. Palm and fruit trees were few and far between; they were surrounded mostly by rocks and shrubs. It was only mid-morning but already, the Captain had shed his new robe from Bethlehem, as well as his jacket and knitted waistcoat. He loosened the collar of his damp shirt and gave it a flap. Paulo had his overalls unzipped to the waist revealing a plain white t-shirt underneath.

"What would happen if we tried to get back into the city?" asked Paulo.

"We'd be sent straight out again. We're not allowed there anymore. Ha! Trust *me* to get banished from the 'holy city'."

"What's to stop us going to another city?"

"Some nice weather and some transport mostly. But that's what banished people probably end up doing." The Captain cupped his hands around his mouth and called, "Hello!!"

They waited a moment, but could only hear the whistle of the hot breeze in their ears.

"There's no one around," said Paulo.

"Hey, there's nothing that isn't shown that you can see... or something like that."

"...What?"

"Well we haven't looked everywhere yet, so how do you know there's nobody around? They didn't drive us all *that* far from the city. There'd be travellers..."

"We could easily get lost, there's not much in the way of landmarks."

The Captain stopped in his tracks. Looking a little way ahead to a dark lump on the ground, he said grimly, "I would say *that's* quite a distinct landmark, wouldn't you?"

They approached cautiously. Paulo swallowed and said worriedly, "Is he... is he dead?"

The Captain knelt beside the motionless body lying on his stomach in the dust. He put two fingers up to the poor man's neck to find a pulse, but there wasn't one. He stood up again. "I'd say for at least a couple of hours."

"Captain," Paulo then said as he spotted another lump further ahead. Another poor soul in the same state. "What do you think they died of? Thirst? Heat stroke?"

"I doubt if anyone who... wait a minute."

"What?"

"What do you notice about both of them? What do they have in common?"

"Apart from the obvious?"

"Apart from the obvious," the Captain nodded.

"Erm... they... both... um... I give up."

"They're both facing the same way. As if they were both travelling in the same direction before they collapsed. They also have purplish skin..."

"Well what is it over there they were so desperate to get to?" Paulo pointed in the direction he and the Captain had come from.

"Or," said the Captain darkly, "what was it in *that* direction," he pointed the opposite way, "that they were so desperate to get *away* from?"

They both looked in *that* direction. Paulo felt a shiver run down his spine, even though he was sweltering.

They started walking onward.

Back in Jerusalem, Marius had been acting as if nothing had happened the night before. He and his family were lounging around having cheerful conversations. But every time Evie passed the group, she noticed that Marius was never fully interested in the discussion. He was always frowning. Evie suspected his occasional nods were just to make it look like he was listening.

It was the first time Evie saw Marius properly in the full light of day. His hair was black and cropped close to his head. He had fat, stubby fingers and wore the usual Roman clothes, but it struck her that something was not quite right about him.

Evie wanted to stay well clear of him, but she was called out into the courtyard where they were lounging. As soon as she appeared, she could feel Marius' eyes on her. She felt small and exposed. She wished she could give him an intimidating look that said *I'm on to you,* but those eyes of his were too scary to look into for any longer than a second.

Marius spoke. "Let me look at her. Yes... yes, she looks strong enough. Strong-willed if nothing else. And young. That is what I want, a young servant. Someone who will be able to serve me for years to come."

What is he talking about?

Then Lucius spoke. "You're telling me you want to buy the girl from me?"

Evie's eyes widened. *Buy me? Is this legal?*

"Yes. For a good price of course."

Evie panicked. *I can't be bought. I'm a person!*

"But Lucius, we've only just acquired her," said Cassia. "I like her and I want to keep her."

Evie gave a subtle little nod, happy that Cassia was putting forward her opinion.

"We don't want emotions to get in the way dear," said Lucius. "We haven't heard how much Marius is willing to pay. Living where we live, you can have any servant you want."

Evie had Lucius on one side of her and Marius on the other, and she looked from one to the other, hoping Cassia would speak up more.

"Evie is inexperienced," Cassia said. "You wouldn't want to have her. She is still learning."

Yeah, you tell him Cassia!

"She's in good enough shape for me," said Marius. "Any other slave will already have stripes on his back and worn-out joints."

"What if I said she's not for sale?" said Cassia.

Evie nodded again and smiled.

Lucius put a hand up to his wife to shush her. "What price would you offer?"

Evie frowned again and looked at Marius, waiting for his answer.

He eventually said, "Fifteen denarii."

Evie's eyebrows rose. She didn't really understand what a denarii was, but to hear herself being put down to a price felt weird and appalling. She felt like merely one of those drab old robes in the Bethlehem marketplace.

"Marius," said Portia, his wife, "we don't need another slave, what's the meaning of this?"

Ignoring her, Marius said to Lucius, "What do you say to that?"

"No sale. I think the girl is worth more than that." (Evie gave a satisfied nod.) "Thirty denarii."

She frowned. *Darn it.* It wasn't over.

"Twenty," said Marius.

"Thirty. I will settle for no less."

Yeah Lucius, you stick to your guns!

Marius sat back. He stroked his beard and

breathed out a long, steady breath from his nostrils. Then he looked at Lucius straight in the eyes. "I will give you twenty-five denarii... *and* my other slave for her."

Evie's jaw uncontrollably dropped. She gave a hopeful glance at Lucius, waiting for his response. *Come on, say no! No deal!*

But Lucius was thinking about it.

Portia said, "Marius no. What are you saying? I don't want to give Levi away. He's a good worker."

"He'll be a good worker for your sister."

"But Marius," said Lucius, "we seem to be getting the better deal here. You would exchange your strong male slave for someone as weak and inexperienced as this girl?"

Marius would not take his eyes off Lucius. He maintained a burning, intimidating, relentless stare. "Whatever it takes."

Portia's nostrils flared, but she remained silent from now on. Apparently she knew when to stop pushing her husband.

Evelyn was looking at Lucius too, with a heavy breath and a pounding heart. She'd given up on Cassia. *Don't say yes. Don't say yes. Please don't say yes.*

Lucius shrugged slowly. "Alright, but I don't

understand you."

Evie's shoulders sagged. Her mouth went dry.

"Let me have your mark of agreement." Marius leaned forward, holding out his hand.

Lucius shook it, practically right in front of Evie's face, and although she'd just been bought with a price, she suddenly felt worthless.

CHAPTER
14

COMING CLEAN

The next thing Evie knew, there was talk of Lucius and Cassia leaving. She was confused as they hadn't planned to return home for another few days yet. Levi confirmed it when he spoke to her while she was hanging up some wet rags to dry.

"This evening?" said Evie, frowning. Why?"

"Do not ask of me," he shrugged.

"Will you be... sad to leave your home?"

Levi shrugged. "It is Marius' home. It is Marius' life I've been living."

"You know what I mean. You've been here for so long, it's like a home."

"I suppose so," he said, softening a little. "But I'm hoping it will be a nice change. Surely any master could not be as harsh as Marius."

"Harsh?" Evie's stomach squirmed.

"I do not wish to frighten you, but I am glad it is you who is staying and I who is leaving."

"Marius really mean, huh?"

"Doesn't care for anybody but himself. Sometimes I don't even think he cares for his wife. And if it is that way for the mistress, what treatment for the slave?" Levi left to continue his duties.

Nice way of showing you don't wish to frighten me. But even though she was frightened, Evie remembered that there was something more to Marius than what was on the surface. *That machine he's keeping secret from the world for a start. Is he even from this time himself?*

Someone in the wrong time?
I would never have dreamt of such a thing, but now that I know time travel is real...

Maybe it's a good thing you're staying here. Perhaps you could get to the bottom of it all.
Get my 'Nancy Drew' on and do some sleuthing.
Exactly!

Cassia found Evie and pulled her aside before they had to rush off. She said apologetically, "I didn't want to sell you to Marius but he was so persistent, that brute of a man. And Lucius is always interested in a profit where he can find one."

"Why are you leaving so soon?"

"Something about the weather turning bad apparently and so travelling will be harder."

"Did Marius say that? How can he tell what the weather's gonna be like?" Evie wasn't sure about weather forecasting in ancient times, but she knew they certainly didn't have any convenient T.V. weather channels.

"I do not know. Marius is an influential and intelligent man, I find it difficult to contradict him."

"What if he's just making it up?"

"Why would he?"

"Because..." *Because Marius doesn't trust me and wants to keep his secret safe.* She couldn't say that. It was probably unwise. Anything she'd done to try and make things better so far had only gotten her into trouble. "...I don't know."

A short time later, when Evie heard the clattering of the mare trotting away outside, she'd assumed everyone was out there, and that the house was empty. She jumped when she realised Marius was standing at the other end of the room, leaning against the wall, staring at her.

He didn't move a muscle when she jumped. Just stood there with his arms folded. Evie plucked up some courage and asked, "Why did you pay so much to keep me here?"

"I don't trust you."

"I thought so.

"There is a saying. Keep your friends close, but keep your enemies closer."

Evie's eyebrows twitched inwards. She didn't like the idea of being his enemy. She chose to try and stay out of trouble, so her next words were: "Well is... is there anything you want me to do... at the moment?"

"Go and get a bowl of water, cloths and some soap," he said and then walked away.

In another part of the house, Portia came back inside saying, "I can't believe the change of weather that you predict. How do you know these things?"

"Because my dear," replied Marius, "I know everything." He kissed her head.

"That's no explanation. And a new slave? Why did you go and do that?"

"Well... I thought wives were supposed to submit to their husbands."

"I'm only asking for a reason. You do have one, don't you?"

"That's my business, woman."

"I am your wife, not another of your slaves."

"Don't you need to go to the market?"

"I already did that, early this morning."

"Well go and tend to the garden then, before the day is out."

Portia contained her anger and went out to the garden where she felt happier anyway, leaving Marius alone in the house with Evie.

The household's new servant came and met him with what he'd asked for. She watched him take off his sandals and he said, "Now you will wash my feet."

Evie's nose uncontrollably crinkled up as she looked down at his sweaty, dirty feet. Hairy toes and all. An unintended "ughh," came out of her mouth.

Marius hovered his hand over the handle of a whip that was hanging from his belt and growled, "You are lucky your back is not slashed with stripes for sneaking around where you were not invited. You are mine now. You will do as I say."

Evie glanced at the whip. The thick, braided cords wound around a worn leather handle. She could just about feel the lashes, imagine the constant stinging on her back. It was either that or wash this dude's feet.

Marius plonked down on a lounge of cushions.

Evie knelt opposite him with the bowl and the cloths. He dumped his feet in, and she gingerly put her hands in the bowl, wetting the cloth. It was the weirdest, creepiest thing she'd ever done in her life and it was the most awkward silence that could ever exist. It became worse when he started talking to her.

"You're not from here are you?"

Evie shook her head.

"Where are you from?"

"Bethlehem."

He made one quick exhale of air – a chuckle. He folded his arms and reclined back. "Where were you born? You don't look Jewish."

Evie hated lying. She hated that hot prickly flush that waved like a red flag all over her face, while hoping the listener somehow wouldn't notice. She tried to get away with telling as much truth as possible. "I wasn't born in Bethlehem."

"So? Where?"

"Far away." *How silly*, she thought. *That sounded deliberately secretive.* "I mean... it's a distant... *small* town. You wouldn't know it."

By the look on his face, she could tell he was still expecting an answer.

She hoped he hadn't heard of it. Who could tell *what* this guy knew. "...Adelaide."

He sat back, thinking. It didn't look like he'd heard of Adelaide, thankfully. "You haven't always been a slave."

"No. In fact right up until two days ago I was a free, normal person."

"Yes, Portia's sister said something about that." He seemed to be in his own little world of thought.

"Where are *you* from?" Evie decided to see if she could use his distractedness to ask *him* a few questions.

It clearly took him off guard. "That is none of your business."

"It's just I've seen quite a few Roman people now, and to me, you don't look Roman." *That's it,* she thought. *That's what's odd about him.*

"You're talking nonsense."

"I think it's your nose."

"Do you have no fear, girl?"

Evie was very much afraid, but trying not to show it. Apparently, she was doing a good job of that. She saw no harm in lying about this one. "Nup." She was dying to talk more about the machine downstairs, but she remembered his words last night: *You will not speak of or even think any more of this... or I will have to get rid of you.* She had no idea what this man was capable of, and she didn't fancy finding out.

Perhaps if she had some leverage. Something

that might frighten *him* a bit. He was not the sort of creature you'd imagine being frightened of anything, but there had to be something. What would *his* fear be? She realised she already knew that answer. *People finding out about his secret.* Lots of people. Powerful people. Perhaps if she could make him believe that he was in trouble with some of these powerful people...

"I'll tell you the truth," Evie suddenly heard herself saying, nerves going bonkers in her stomach.

Marius waited, one eyebrow raised.

She lowered her voice a little. "We're very interested in what you have downstairs and I'm... *we* are going to find it difficult to forget about it."

Marius looked unconvinced. "Who is *we*?"

"I have some friends who are on their way to find me and they're going to agree with me when I say that... King Herod... no, Emperor *Caesar* should be informed."

"Who are your friends?" he said sceptically.

What to say? What to say? "...That's not for you to know."

"You're playing games with me, girl. And that is a big mistake. You will live to regret it. In fact, you may not even live at all. Do you comprehend?"

Evie tried not to look scared. She tried to

117

arrange her facial features into a confident smile –
as if there was some big joke that Marius didn't
know about.

But Marius did not look phased. He looked
calmer and smugger than ever. And then suddenly
he stood up in one sharp motion, causing
the bowl of soapy water
to tip over, splashing
it everywhere. Evie
jumped backwards
onto her feet and kept
backing away as he moved towards her. *Well, that
didn't work.*

"You don't believe I will stay true to my word;
about getting rid of you. But I can and I will."

"Y-you'll go to jail for that, won't you?"

"Ha!" He brought his hand once again down to
the handle on his hip and unhooked the whip.
Evie's stomach twanged. She backed away from
him, but soon realised she had backed herself into
a corner.

Marius straightened out the whip so that he was
holding the handle in one hand and the end of the
cords in the other in front of her.

"Please don't," she said softly.

"Tell me everything then," he said calmly. "Or

soon you will wish I'd killed you before."

"I can't. I'm nobody really."

"Ah, you've changed your tune."

He reached out one of his giant hands, grabbed her by the arm, and turned her so that her back was facing him. She sprung off one foot to try and make a run for it. He grabbed for her, but he only gripped her robe, so as she escaped from the corner, it left him standing there holding her outer robe. He stared at her wide-eyed and open-mouthed.

What's happened? Why is he looking at me like that? Evie saw her robe in his hand. Her jeans, pink t-shirt, and white hoody were all revealed. She looked down at her clothes and then back up at Marius.

It wasn't Lucius' confused bewilderment, as though he was looking at something he'd never seen before. Instead, a nasty smile crept onto Marius' face and he whispered, "Of *course.*"

15

THE PURPLE PREDATOR

Evie ran. But once outside, she had no idea where to go. It was that split-second hesitation that let her down. Marius caught hold of her arm. She struggled and struggled to pull free but Marius' hand was a clamp. Then he gripped her shoulders, whisked her around and inspected her face closely. His lip twitched, "It *is* you. Evie..."

Just then, Portia called from a distance. "Marius! There are some people here to see you."

Evie and Marius looked at each other. Evie hoped and prayed it was the Captain and Paulo, and Marius wasn't going to take any chances. He hauled her back into the house and headed straight to the closed door. She was tossed inside and carried all the way down to the bottom. Then Marius quickly grabbed some rope, tied her wrists up in it and bound it to the sconce on the wall above her head. When he spoke, his breath made her eyelids blink, "Finally I can have some revenge."

"R-r-revenge?"

"Because of you and that wretched prophesy of the sky-blue overalls, I'm stuck here! So now I'm going to stick *you* here and see how you like it." He stood up, laughed out loud, and then disappeared back up the steps, leaving the place in total darkness.

The Captain and Paulo had followed a trail of bodies across the wilderness until they came to the edge of a sea of flourishing, purpley-green undergrowth. "As I thought," said the Captain grimly.

When Paulo could find his voice, he muttered in disbelief, looking out onto the expanse of deadly ground. "Kratilier Lumis." He looked up at the Captain and said, "We can't dig all this up."

The Captain shook his head. "Perhaps we could burn it."

"What about the fumes?"

He shook his head again. "Fumes should be

harmless. We just need a match. There's been no rain out here, it'll be as dry as a fish, if the fish had been left out of the water on a pier in the sun."

"O...kay, but how do you suppose we find a match?" said Paulo, looking around.

"I don't. Especially seeing as they haven't been invented yet."

"Well I learnt how to start a fire with stones when I was a kid," said Paulo.

"So did I. But have you seen any appropriate flint stones lying around?"

Paulo shook his head, hopelessly. "Haven't you got some gadget that could do the trick? I mean you've got things like your Atom Relocating Molecular Teleport Device, your Portable Audio Clandestine Digital Communicator..."

The Captain clicked his finger loudly. "Of course, I forgot! I have my Manual Hand Operating Fuel Injected Flame Combustion Apparatus. Paulo, you're a genius."

"What's that?"

"It should be somewhere..." The Captain dug around in his pockets. First his trousers, then all the pockets in the coat draping on his arm, and he eventually pulled out a small, shiny object. When he flicked his thumb down one corner of it with a click, a flame ignited from the top.

"A lighter?"

"Oh is that what you call it? I suppose that's more efficient. And... you know, quicker."

The Captain lit his Manual Hand Operating Fuel Injected Flame Combustion Apparatus, knelt down and held the flame up to a leaf of the Violet Assassin. "Come on, come on," he muttered. "Catch light." It caught, and there was a tiny flame dancing on the tip of that one leaf. They watched it in anticipation...

...until the flame dwindled and snuffed out leaving only a swirl of smoke disappearing into the air. The leaf looked unaffected. Paulo frowned. "That's not supposed to happen is it?"

"I'd better try again." The Captain knelt again and repeated steps one to three. In dismay, they watched the flame die again, leaving the leaf perfectly unscorched. "Well," he said, standing up and putting the lighter back in his pocket. "You learn something new everyday. Kratilier Lumis does not burn."

"But there must be some way to control it. Otherwise, that forest where you said it grows must be riddled with the stuff."

"That's it!" said the Captain, grabbing Paulo's shoulders. "You're a double genius! The forest!"

"What about it?"

"Fact is, the forest is *not* riddled with it. There's some natural process there that keeps it under control. All I have to do is figure out what it is."

"But how? Go to the forest?"

"In a sense. I'll look it up."

"Look it up? How?"

"On my databank. All we need to do is find the Train!" he said cheerfully.

Paulo's shoulders sank. "So we're back where we started. Finding the Train."

"Well we always needed to find the Train," he shrugged and smiled.

CAPTAIN!!

The Captain inclined his head. "Listen."

Paulo frowned. "Is someone calling you?"

The Captain said chirpily, as though he was answering a telephone call, "Hello? Yes?"

"CAPTAIN!!!" cried the voice. "PAULO!!!"

They scanned the landscape carefully, and soon Paulo spotted a horse in the distance galloping towards them. "Over there!"

"Please! Help me!" the rider called. They ran towards him, saw the bronze armour, a blaze of red. It was a Roman soldier. When they met him, he coughed out, "Thank the gods!" He slid off the horse, collapsing into a heap on the ground with his crimson cloak draped over him.

The Captain quickly stooped over and rolled him onto his side. "It's Silius!" He saw the spread of purple rash in the corner of his mouth straight away.

"I didn't believe you about the plant," Silius coughed and spluttered. "But now I apologise..."

"Shhh," said the Captain, placing a hand on his forehead and giving him a general check over. "It's alright. What you need now is an antidote."

"Is there one?" said Paulo.

"I touched the plant in the bag," Silius wheezed.

"Yes, it's alright. Let's think forward. Since something foreign has entered your system, something non-foreign might fix it up."

"How do you know?" asked Paulo.

"I don't know for sure, but it works with some things. Only we must work fast."

"What is there we can use?" Paulo asked.

"Well, he has to actually consume it... I know! The fruit trees! I think they're figs. Paulo, run over and pick a fig will you?"

125

Paulo obeyed while the Captain tried to keep Silius calm and conscious. He seemed to want to lay his head down and go to sleep but the Captain knew that if he fell asleep, it might be forever. "Silius, I know you want to rest, but you have to stay with me! Erm... what's the day of the week?"

"I don't know," he said breathlessly. "My mind's gone blank, my head feels fuzzy."

"Okay tell me what it feels like. Your throat, tell me exactly what it feels like in your throat."

"Like there is a fungus growing... inside my mouth and around my lips. Itchy. And crawling."

"Paulo! Hurry up with that fig!"

"It's here!" said Paulo, rushing down beside the Captain, sending a whirl of dust into the air. "I brought a few."

"Right Silius, eat this."

"No, I can't. Can't feel my mouth anymore."

"You must. It might just be your salvation."

Silius grabbed the Captain's hand with the fig in it and took as big-a-bite as he could manage.

"Please let this work," mumbled the Captain.

"What should it do?" asked Paulo.

"The cells inside the fruit might work as antibodies to fight the cells of the Violet Assassin which are attacking his body. Besides give him a few extra vitamins at the same time."

126

Silius took more and more bites of the fig. Once he was done with one, he started on another, and thick pink juice ran through his beard.

"How do you feel?" asked the Captain.

"It feels... better, I think. And tingly."

The Captain smiled. "The antioxidants are reacting with the poison. Keep eating!"

"This is delicious," said Silius, sitting up. "And I can feel every part of my mouth again... It's Tuesday."

The Captain let out a huge joyful laugh, looking up at the sky. "Thank you."

"Praise the gods," said Silius, still a little weak.

"The God of figs perhaps. Can you stand up?"

"Yes, I think so."

Paulo saw that the purple rash had faded a little. "We should hang on to these figs."

"Good idea," said the Captain. Then he looked at the horse that had carried the soldier here and patted it on the neck. "I recognise you! You're one of Elisha's faithful friends. Good to see you again."

"The other one," Silius said, a little breathlessly and dusting himself off, "is still at the palace. A thousand pardons again, Captain... whoever you are. I now realise how dangerous that plant was."

"Well there's a lot more around the place that still needs to be dealt with."

"Where has it come from?"

"Somewhere else," said Paulo, using the Captain's words from earlier.

"Another city?"

"Well, a little further than that," said the Captain.

"What can be done about it?" asked Silius. "If it's not controlled soon, it will be like a plague."

"I need to find something that belongs to me. And then I'll be able to start coming up with a plan."

"Tell me what it is, and I will help you. I'll take you back to Jerusalem if that is what you need. I can provide you with a pardon."

The Captain sighed and pulled out a gadget from one of his pockets. This time, it was a small circular shaped thing, not much bigger than the lighter.

"What is it this time," Paulo asked, looking at the small, black disk.

"Nothing," he said. "Absolutely nothing. I should have been getting signals from this thing. I hope it's not broken." He gave it a gentle shake.

"What is it?"

"It's a Unique Radio-Wave-Operated Link Chip. I own two. Two that are actively linked anyway. The other one is inside the Train. They send signals to each other, allowing me to locate the

Train if I ever forget where I parked it. Very handy in shopping centre car parks."

Paulo was astonished. "Then why, for goodness sake, didn't you bring it out earlier?"

"I did. I just didn't tell you about it, because I was hoping to spare you from the bad news."

"Bad news?"

"There was no signal when we were back in Bethlehem. And there's still no signal now."

"So the one on the Train has conked out?"

"It's unlikely, these are very hardy things. It would be more likely for the Train to have gone out of exis..." the Captain's eyes widened as a revelation dawned on him... "...out of existence."

"What? The Train... doesn't exist? How can that be?"

"Believe me. It's possible."

16

THE RETURN OF A FAITHFUL FRIEND

"What if we go back to Jerusalem like Silius offered?" Paulo asked the Captain.

"But what do we do once we get there?" said the Captain, more so to himself.

"You usually *answer* the questions, Captain."

"Well, it's like longing for something like... success, or riches, or the next Beatles album to come out. When you finally get there, you think... now what? You find it hasn't satisfied you like you thought it would. Actually, that part's not like the Beatles. They were never disappointing. Except maybe *Revolution 9*. That was weird. Even for me, who has a very high 'weirdness' threshold."

"Captain you're off topic."

"Sorry! Look, our best chance is in a busy city where we can talk to people. But... perhaps we should first deal with all this Violet Assassin out here. But finding the Train leads to a more permanent solution..."

"I've never seen you so indecisive Captain."

"That's because I'm hardly ever indecisive... or maybe it's because you haven't known me for very long. I can't decide which."

"Maybe we could let the king know, this Herod guy, about the Violet Assassin..."

"The authorities are not bothered about what happens to those who have been banished," said Silius. "When the government banishes anyone, it washes its hands of them."

"That's it!" the Captain said, snapping his fingers.

"You want to go to the king?" said Paulo.

"No, no, that won't do any good. What Silius said about washing its hands... you know Silius, you're not as silly-ous as you look."

"What do you mean?"

"Sorry, didn't mean to call you silly. Only... perhaps in that helmet... anyway, no! *Kings,* this heat! *Focus!* Wash its hands, like you were 'washed' in a sense of the Violet Assassin. We'll wash the Violet Assassin itself!"

131

"Wash the Violet Assassin?"

"Since I don't have my Train's databank for the moment, we can improvise. Now, this fruit not only stopped Silius from dying, it reversed the whole process. What if we make a big bath of the stuff, you know, juice it down and drench the plant in it... What do you think?"

"I think we're in for some more walking," Paulo said tiredly.

"Do you think it would work?" said Silius.

"No idea! But it's worth a try. We need to pick as many figs as we can find."

Paulo couldn't help it, but he let out a little sigh.

"Come on! Where's your enthusiasm?" The Captain grabbed both Silius and Paulo around the shoulders and squeezed them. "Here's our chance to save the world again!"

What good am I to anyone now? Evie complained to herself down in the darkness of the underground room. *I had to go and open my big mouth, didn't I?*

Better than slaving away upstairs?

I suppose I could look at it that way.

And you didn't get whipped.

True.

And you're still alive.

I guess I have lots to be thankful for.

Evie took a deep breath. She wondered what Marius meant about revenge. And about the sky-blue overalls. *Paulo* was wearing sky-blue overalls. But what did *he* have to do with some prophesy?

For the moment, that question was far too hard. Evie decided to think about where she was instead. *I am technically where I wanted to be... with this machine to find out more about it... but I can't see it, and I can't reach it.* She sighed out loud.

Getting out of here would still be my first preference.

Thought about praying?

"Well it's worked before," she said to herself. "Dear Lord, thank you that You've kept me safe and unharmed... mostly. I pray that You protect Paulo and the Captain as well, that they'll find me down here, and that we can get the Train back... somehow..." she stopped, staring into the blackness in front of her, thinking about the Train.

Now that her eyes had adjusted a little, she could see a subtle glow from the centre of the room. *I might be able to reach it with my feet if I stretched out...* She shuffled her lower half away

133

from the wall, as far as it could go without lifting off the ground. Then she stretched out her legs, until every muscle in them was aching, and flayed them around. Then all of a sudden, her foot caught on something, there was a scrape sound, and then a huge **CLATTER** and **THUD!** Evie gasped and froze for a moment, pretty certain she had just made the machine fall to the floor. She looked around wide-eyed in the darkness, hoping desperately that no one upstairs had heard anything, and that the machine hadn't been damaged. All was silent, and she started to breathe again. But hang on, no it wasn't silent. There was a soft hum in the room now. The machine seemed to come alive. *Whoops. Have I turned it on?*

She still couldn't properly reach it, so she wriggled her wrists in the ropes and realised they felt looser than before. She twisted them to and fro between the ropes, expanding and contracting what muscles she had there to loosen the ropes more. It was working a little bit, but not enough to slip her hands out. *But if it's worked a bit, then it can work some more…*

Evie's patience was tested. The time it took for her to wriggle free from the ropes was much longer than the time it has taken you to read this sentence, but when she did, she stood up and rubbed her sore wrists. That little glow, now at floor level, was the only thing she could see in the darkness, so she went right up to it and felt around in its general area. Closer up, she could make out the rough shape of it. *How can there be a light?* she wondered. *Solar Power?* It seemed incredible considering it was 4 B.C.

It seemed to have landed upright. She began to wonder if she'd be able to get that image of the Train up again in the empty space framed by the wires and tubes. She tried to remember what Marius had done, just before it appeared the last time. She felt her fingers around the shapes of the machine. And before she knew it, she'd pressed some sort of button and there was a **CLUNK**!

Oooh... what have I done?

The machine started rattling worryingly. *Have I activated a self-destruct or something?* she thought with horror. As it kept on rattling and jiggling, she backed away slowly towards the stairs. If it was going to self-destruct she'd have to run for it... and then get in huge trouble with Marius for not only getting free, but for blowing up his machine. *But you can't self-destruct! I need you to get the Train back!* she screamed inside her head.

Just as she crept backwards up onto the first step of the passageway, there was another loud **CLUNK**! And then just the quiet humming again. Evie looked back at the machine. Something had happened. She crept back towards it cautiously, eyes fixed on the space surrounded by the wires and pipes.

"The Train!" she uttered. A picture of it anyway, and once again, she didn't need the special glasses. She could see its deep green sides, the huge wheels, smokestack, carriage windows along the side and the little cursive logo, *Blackerby,* on the cylindrical boiler. It was definitely the Captain's Train. "There you are," she said fondly, crouching down to look closely. "You might have just saved my life." *But where are you, actually? Are you... inside this thing... somehow?*

She raised her hand up to it. Her fingers passed straight through. *Just an image...* She noticed a dull light gently flashing on the machine underneath. She had a feel of a little knob where the light was coming from. Turns out the knob was a button. And, although you might expect her to have learnt her lesson from pushing unknown buttons, she pushed it, and the machine rumbled again. But it was over in a second, and then a momentary concentration of blue light descended to the left of the machine that, for a split second, seemed to take the shape of the Train. Then it was gone, and the room was back to its usual darkness.

I wonder, Evie thought, and she walked quickly over to where the blue glow had been. She held her arms out in front of her.* Her fingers collided with the smooth paintwork of the Train. That wonderful, magical machine. A rescue ship out on a rough, stormy ocean. A familiar and faithful friend.

The Train.

She wondered if she could get inside it. But when she found her way to the door, it was locked and only the Captain had a key.

There was an incessant beeping out in the wilderness where the Captain, Paulo and Silius were busily searching for more fig trees.

Beep... beep... beep... beep...

"We've got lots," said Paulo, running out of breath. "But we'll need millions to make enough juice to soak that field of Kratilier Lumis!"

"Kratoolia Whomis?" said Silius.

---

* the way people tend to do when they're pretending to be a ghost, (although, to be quite honest, I've never seen a ghost walk this way).

137

"The Violet Assassin."

Beep... beep... beep... beep...

"Could we dilute it?" asked Silius.

"A good idea," said the Captain, "but it might not be strong enough. We should do a test."

Beep... beep... beep... beep...

"These look just perfect for juicing, my Aunt Ezzie would say," said the Captain.

Beep... beep... beep... beep...

"Now to juice them," he continued. "We'll have to ah... we need something to juice them in... er... what *is* that beeping noise?"

"It's coming from your pocket!" Paulo answered.

"Is it? Oh!" the Captain exclaimed, as if in sudden realisation. He dug deep down in his trouser pocket and whipped out the Unique Radio-Wave-Operated Link Chip. He stared at it for a few seconds, gave it a shake, and then laughed out loud.

"What? What is it?" said Paulo.

"The Train! It exists! It's come back into space and time!"

"Does that mean someone's been flying it?"

"I don't know. I don't know how, what, when, where, who, or why. All I know is, the signal's back and I can track it now. Which means I do know *where*, ignore what I said earlier. All we have to do

138

is follow this signal. It's in..." he held the gadget up as though it was a compass, turned around a little way and then stopped. "...that direction."

"What about the fruit?" said Paulo. "And the Violet Assassin?"

"Let's not let our efforts go to waste. How would you two feel about staying here and continuing the juicing project while I go and track down the Train?"

Paulo nodded. "Alright but..."

"But we should decide where to meet."

"How about outside the palace?" said Silius.

"Are you sure we won't get arrested again?" the Captain said, starting off.

"I will make sure of it," nodded Silius.

The Captain smiled gratefully. "Right... And of course, if you happen to run into Evelyn... you know, bring her along too."

17

GETTING ACQUAINTED

In the deep, musty gloom, Evelyn was sitting on the floor, leaning up against the invisible side of the Train. Even though she couldn't get in, it still comforted her, knowing it was right there behind her. She folded her arms and whistled *Jingle Bells* to herself. Evie was not the best whistler. Her attempt sounded more like puffing with the odd out-of-tune note making its way into a sound wave every now and then – sometimes two in a row.

When she'd reached the third chorus, she heard a sound way up at the top of the steps. She strained her ears to hear. It was footsteps. One *pit* after another *pat* down the steps. Her whistling petered out. She ran over to where she had been tied up, sat down on the ground, but then got up again to heave the machine back up on its little table. Then she sat back down again and put her hands up over her head, pretending she hadn't escaped at all – just in case she could trick him.

Each footstep was synchronised with her heartbeat, pulsing loudly in her head.

No, she thought. What if Marius came down here in a fit of rage with his whip or went straight for her throat? *In fact, he probably will as soon as he finds out I've stuffed around with his machine. I'll be defenceless if I just sit here.*

She quickly hopped up onto her feet again and darted around the dark room, looking for something to arm herself with. A stick, a log, a piece of machine equipment... a frying pan, a cricket bat...

There was nothing. She thought of the heavy spade inside the Train that she'd used to shovel fuel into its firebox. *If only I had the key!*

Then, beyond the Train she saw a broken chair! It wasn't the best weapon of self-defence, it looked a bit brittle, but it would have to do. Evie flattened herself up against the jagged stone wall, holding the chair up above her head. A heat wave throbbed through her body. The butterflies inside her stomach spread all over, making her legs feel weak.

She tried to plan what her next move was. Make a run for it, find the Captain... She visualised actually smacking the chair down on Marius' head – hard enough to knock him out. *Would I have the strength to do that? Would I have the guts?* She'd never deliberately injured anyone before. And if she did do it, should she even leave him alone down here with the Train?

There was no more time to think about it. Marius had reached the bottom step. As soon as she saw the tip of his sandal land on the ground, she stepped forward, gathered all her strength and brought the chair down on top of his head as hard as she could. She winced, almost imagining the pain on her own head, and then watched Marius stumble, surprised and unbalanced, down onto his knees. She gasped for breath....

Run. The next step in her little plan was *run!* But she was stunned for a moment at what she had done, and then there was the bigger shock. Marius was still moving. He had let out a little grunt on the impact, but now he was getting himself back onto his feet and Evie had just lost her chance to get away. Marius had been quick to grab her wrist and he held on to it so tightly, Evie almost lost all feeling in her hand.

It was a reflex to say, "Let me go!" but she knew there was no reason why he would. With his free hand, he grabbed the chair leg she was holding and threw it across the room. It missed his machine but hit something hard – and it wasn't the wall.

"You wretched girl!" he growled. "Did you think you could conquer me with your puny strength?"

Evie had felt quite pleased with herself that she was able to at least knock him to the floor, even though it was probably the element of surprise, not the element of strength that did it.

"You're proving to be a nuisance!"

"Yes! I'm a terrible nuisance! Why don't you just let me go?"

He pulled out a weapon that had been concealed somewhere inside his clothes. She would have expected a dagger, a whip or a rope or something. But it was a pistol. He sneered, "Because *Evie*, if I let you go, then..." He suddenly frowned and went silent. His eyes slowly shifted over to where he'd thrown the chair leg. Then his head turned, and his body followed. Still holding Evie tightly by the wrist, he stepped into the middle of the room. "...I threw this against the wall." He picked up the chair leg again. "But it's here." He straightened, reached out his hand and touched

143

something.

Evie squinted her eyes shut.

"What is *that* doing here?" he said in a low, angry growl.

"What? I don't see anything," she said quickly, wide-eyed, trying not to look guilty.

He lifted the chair leg again and jabbed it forward, hitting the invisible barrier.

"Don't, you'll scratch it!" she blurted.

"I knew it," he said with the slightest, sly smile. "This is yours. Yours and..." he made a small, barely audible laugh. "Well well."

"What?"

"It all makes sense now. You're not a very good time traveller. With your clothes and your manner of speech."

"Well what about you and your gun? They're not supposed to be around for... for decades... centuries. What are you doing with *that*, let alone this machine? Where and when are *you* from?" Evie surprised herself; she even plucked up enough courage to yank her wrist out of his grasp and dig her hands into her waist.

"How did you materialise this machine?"

"I don't know I... just pressed a few buttons on *your* machine."

"Do you realise this is a very dangerous piece of

equipment for someone who doesn't know what they're doing?"

"Yeah... I thought it was going to blow up at one stage."

"You fool."

"What do you want with the Train anyway? What was it doing inside your machine?"

"How quaint. To call it a train, because it looks like one."

"It doesn't just look like one, it *is* one."

"You'll be well advised to remember that you are still a slave in this house. You will speak when you are spoken to." He took a step towards her. "Now listen very carefully. I need this space and time ship to get away from this place and get my life back. You will take me to *the Captain* and he will give me the secrets of how it works. Understand?"

She looked up at him with her big, dark brown eyes. A chuckle from the back of her throat came out. "That's not going to happen."

Marius' face fired up again and he held up his gun close to her face.

"Wait," she said, "how do you know about the Captain?"

Marius was taken by surprise. "How do you *not* know that... ah... time travel. I'm still getting used to it myself. None of it's happened for you yet."

145

"What are you talking about?"

"Just tell me his name. Mortimer never told me."

"Who's Mortimer? And I don't know his name."

"You lying wretch."

"It's true! I don't know what his name is, he's never told me!"

"You're a stupid creature."

She wished he would stop calling her stupid.

"I think now would be the time to, as the saying goes, say your prayers." He loaded the pistol. "I should have killed you when I first met you anyway."

Evie took a deep breath. She'd said prayers. Plenty of them lately. But they weren't doing any good. But then, what happened next, happened so fast that in the time it takes you to read it, it could have happened ten times over. The gun was flicked out of Marius' hand. It skidded across the floor and he spun away from Evie in surprise. Evie tripped backwards on the other bits of the broken chair and landed painfully on the floor. In the dull light she thought she saw two figures in front of her. One was clearly Marius and the other... when her eyes managed to adjust a little more, she realised was...

"Captain!" she exclaimed with joy and relief. *Or am I hallucinating?* She rubbed her eyes to make sure she wasn't just seeing what she wanted to see.

He stood there, strong and calm, but soon Marius went to wrestle him down. The Captain said, "If that's the way you want it." He took out the Atom Relocating Molecular Teleport Device, pressed a button on it and shoved it into Marius' chest. In reflex, Marius grabbed it, the Captain let go, stepped back, and in the blink of an eye, Marius was gone.

"Banishment for attempted murder... and really bad breath," said the Captain, dusting off his hands.

Evie gazed up with her mouth wide open. The Captain walked forward and held an arm down to her, sporting a big smile.

She took his hand and he hoisted her up onto her feet. Without a word, she hugged him, and tears rolled down her cheeks unashamedly. "You certainly know how to search for someone. How did you find me?" She broke away to look at him.

"As a matter of fact, I haven't found what I'm looking for yet. I was looking for the Train."

"Oh nice. And never mind about me."

"Well, you're an added bonus, obviously."

"You were just in time. He was gonna *kill* me!"

"Yes, who *was* that disagreeable fellow?"

"My master technically. I'm his slave. Oh, there's so much to tell you but... wait, what's happened to him? Where's he gone?"

"I just set my Atom Relocating Molecular Teleport Device for somewhere out in the wilderness where Paulo and I were banished to."

"You and Paulo were banished? Gee we're doing real well, aren't we? Where *is* Paulo?"

"Still there. Now, I need to find the Train. My instrument led me here, which is strange. *Unless*, the Train has developed some sort of... mysterious ability to make a biochemical connection between itself and its passengers. So in leading me to the Train, my Unique Radio-Wave-Operated Link Chip, instead, led me to you." The Captain shook his head in amazement. "I've never discovered that before. The Train could be even more complex than I've thought all this time."

Evie had been listening patiently, but now she finally managed to get a word in. "*Or*... perhaps the Train is here in this room." Evie knew that the Captain often kept his piloting goggles in his right-hand jacket pocket when he wasn't wearing them on his head. She got them out for him and placed them in front of his eyes.

"Ah," said the Captain. "Good."

Paulo and Silius carried a bag full of figs to the sea of Violet Assassin.

"How are we going to juice them?" said Silius.

"With our hands."

"I meant what are we going to juice them into?"

"How about your helmet? Unless... that's against the law?"*

Silius took it straight off and said, "Yes, of course! I mean, no, I don't mind. Let's do it."

They squashed up several figs with their hands into the helmet and once there was a good amount of runny pinky-orangey juice, they poured it over a small area of the plant and waited. There was not really any visible reaction. If anything, it seemed to change colour slightly, but after that, there was nothing. They could have sat there all day and night and nothing would have happened.

"Do you think maybe it's taken out the toxicity?" asked Silius, doubtfully.

"How do you feel about testing that theory?" Paulo said, also doubtfully.

---

* It very well could have been. In the Roman soldier rule book, right after 'do not be cheerful to passersby' and just before 'be sure to mention Caesar when anyone asks thou who thouast barrack for' it might say 'thou must not juice fruit inside thine helmet'.

"Well we could. We have the cure..."

"Look!" Paulo said suddenly, pointing at the plant. But it wasn't an optimistic 'look' at all. The leaves of the plant had returned to their original colour. As if it was repelling any trace of the juice.

"I have a strong feeling," said Paulo, in exhausted disbelief, "that it hasn't worked."

18

THE CAPTAIN'S SECRET ADVENTURE

||||||||||||||||||||||||||||||||||||||||||||||||||||||||||

"So it was *me* that saved my life?" said Evie, stepping up onto an invisible step.

"Yes, you switching on this... thing and bringing the Train back into existence was what led me here. Before that, I couldn't get a signal for the Train." The Captain was examining Marius' machine in the light from the Train carriage. He was fascinated.

"But what even *is* this thing?"

"Well you tell *me*. You're the one who's had a chance to tinker around with it."

"Well there's a button somewhere that turned it on. Then there was a button that made it act like it was gonna blow up, but it didn't because the next thing there was an image of the Train in the middle there... and then there was another button which must have made the Train appear..."

"Interesting," said the Captain. Although he didn't appear to be concentrating on what Evie was saying at all.

"I don't get how you run something like this in ancient times. It looks like it needs electricity. How do you make electricity?"

"Yes, quite possibly," he replied absently.

"Captain, was that your Atom Relocating thing you gave to Marius?"

"Yes it was, yes," he said calmly, finally coming away from the machine and towards the Train.

"But that's bad; now *he* has it. He might destroy it or something."

The Captain shook his head. "He won't destroy it." He nodded back towards the machine. "He's not only interested in technology, he's also very good at it. He'll want to know how it works and keep it for himself." The Captain walked past Evie onto the Train. She followed him through to the engine room.

"Well then what if he tries to steal it?"

"He can't use it for another twenty-four hours and I hope to see him again before then."

Evie shuddered. "I hope I never see him again... although..."

"Although what?"

"Well after a while he... seemed to know me. And he knew about you."

The Captain's lips bunched up on one side. "Mmm."

A picture came up on the monitor which elbowed out from the corner of the Train's control deck. It looked like an Internet search page.

"What are you doing? Googling something?"

"More or less." He typed in some words.

Evie read them out as he did, "Kra... til... lia... loo... lumis. What's that?"

"Something that is endangering the whole of Jerusalem. And beyond."

"Wow. I've missed a lot. I thought as soon as we found the Train, we could just... leave."

"Evelyn, why do you suppose that man had a gun?"

"'Cause he's mean? He's definitely one nasty piece-a-work."

"Wrong. Because he's not from this time."

"Oh yeah, I already worked that out."

"And what's more, he knows you're from a different time too."

"Yeah he does. But how did *you* know?"

The Captain looked at Evie with a raised eyebrow and glanced up and down at her clothes.

153

"Oh yeah. The robe came off when he tried to whip me. What happened to yours?"

"It was hot out in that desert. Did you say he whipped you?"

"No, he was about to. But I ran. But he caught me. But I escaped. But then he caught me again. And then *you* found me! And now here we are... What if he takes off with that thing? What if you don't see him again? That teleport thing's got to be the best thing you own."

"Perhaps," he shrugged. "But mark my words, he'll be wanting to head straight back here."

"Well, I don't know. I'm getting real confused now. Especially now with this... Kratilia Loo Loo thing."

"On the contrary. Put that together with the man with the gun, and it finally all makes sense."

"Well then you must know something I don't."

"I know a lot of things you don't know, but that's not the point."

"Oh and the *coin!*"

"What coin?"

"I found this coin that doesn't belong here either. Get this, it was a coin with ONE SHILLING written on it. From 1934!"

"Ah."

"Except, I thought Marius must have been from

the future. I mean, a further future than when I'm from because of that machine. But then again that wasn't a very futuristic-looking gun. Although I don't know much about guns."

"Mmm," the Captain said again. "Do you have this coin now?"

"No, Felicia snatched it back. She was a slave that I worked with. She's the one who actually found it. She just thought it was pretty."

"Did you hear that?" the Captain suddenly said.

"What?"

"Someone calling out. Are there any other servants here?"

"No, just me. There used to be Levi, but he got sold by Marius along with some denariis or something to buy me."

"So there's no one else here in the house?"

"Um... oh, Marius' wife would be."

"Marius' *wife*?" The Captain seemed confused.

"MARIUS!!"

"I heard it that time," said Evie. "Yeah, that's Portia. She's coming down. She'll see everything!"

"You'd better go and look after her."

"What do I say to her?"

"Tell her... tell her... I don't know, tell her something."

"Oh okay... Mistress, I'm sorry but your

155

husband has been broken up into millions of tiny atoms and reassembled out into the desert somewhere. But don't worry, I'm sure it's only temporary! How does that sound?"

"Fine. Fine," he said, but he was only focused on his computer monitor.

Evie, giving a little sigh of frustration, left the engine room, left the Train, and entered back into the dull underground chamber, soon finding an extremely baffled Portia on the bottom step.

"What is going on here?"

"I... don't really know," said Evie.

"Where's my husband?"

"I don't know... exactly."

"Then what good are you?" she said, walking further into the room. She looked down at the machine. "What is this thing?"

"I... don't know."

Portia's angry eyes locked down onto Evie's wide innocent eyes. "You don't know much, do you? I can tell you what it is *not.*"

"What's that?"

"It's *not* a birthday present."

"Is that what he told you?"

"That is none of your concern."

"Please, let's just get one thing straight," she tried to say politely. "I'm not a slave."

156

"Yes you are. My husband paid good money for you and gave away our only other slave. You belong to us, you stupid girl!"

"I got a 'B-minus' in science last year. I am *not* stupid!"

"What are these nonsense babblings? Find your master for me, I order it."

"But... I can't."

"You can't?" she said, temper rising.

"I can't without actually leaving the city."

"Explain yourself."

"Well, you see he went... out... of the house, and... listen, haven't you been wondering where I was and why no chores have been done? I've been locked down here. Marius tied me up!"

"If you had done something to displease him, then he was right to. I can't think why he wanted to buy you from Lucius. You're completely useless."

"Portia, we think your husband... is from another world. Another *time*." Then Evie had a horrible thought and swallowed. "Unless... you are too."

"What are you raving about?"

Evie felt relieved, perceiving Portia to be earnest. "You're never going to listen to me as long as you see me as a slave, are you?" she mumbled.

Just then, there was a loud sound in the room.

Evie could hardly believe her ears. It was the sound of the Train's engine.

chuff CHOOFETY CHUFF CHOOFETY
chuff CHOOFETY BANG! CHOOFETY
chuff CHOOFETY CHUFF CHOOFETY
chuff CHOOFETY BANG!

"Captain!" she yelled out, running to the space where the Train was supposed to be. The sound was fading. "No!" She reached out to grab the door of the Train, but her body just plummeted straight through to the stone wall behind it.

She paused for a moment with her hands against the wall, thinking. Then she slowly turned, frowning in despair and confusion at the space where the Train should have been.

"Are you out of your mind?" intruded the voice of Portia. "Come here immediately."

Evie did as she was told. All of a sudden, with the Captain gone, she turned back into the timid, frightened little slave-girl.

"Now, I want a straight answer from you. What has happened to my husband?"

"Has your husband been secretive a lot?"

"I demand you answer my questions."

"Does he sometimes disappear down here, and

158

you don't see him for hours?"

Portia froze, staring back at Evie... now listening.

"Does he sometimes use words or talk about things that you don't understand?"

She was silent.

"I'm right, aren't I? Ever wondered why?"

"My husband is a good man. He loves me and... we have no secrets." She was staring at the machine and her voice trailed off.

"How well do you really know him though?"

"I will not put up with this impudence!"

"I don't even know what that means, but I'm trying to help you."

"I do not need to be helped. My marriage is as strong as... as strong as..." she sighed and slumped down on the bottom step. "Oh, I'm so sick of saying that to everybody when it is not true. No one else has ever noticed these things... Just me. No one else sees him the way I do. I can talk to no one. When I tried, no one believed me. He's well respected in this city."

This time, it was Evie who listened.

"He puts on an act. Sometimes in front of me but mostly in front of other people. He pretends to be friendly and considerate; everyone thinks he's wonderful. But there was always something about him that was..."

"Different? Like he doesn't belong here."

"So, he's from a different part of the world. What is so unusual about that?"

"But he calls himself a Roman doesn't he?"

"Yes. Well... I assumed it from the beginning. He did not tell me otherwise. What are you trying to say?"

Evie's shoulders sank. "I don't know, exactly. You ought to talk to the Captain. He'd be able to tell you what's going on."

"Are you saying that my husband is a dangerous man? That he's been living a lie all these years? ...That he doesn't love me?"

"Well, I don't know about that... but I think you're right about him living a lie. And I think that *definitely* he's a dangerous man." She pictured that gun a few inches from her face.

Just then, the sound of the Train engine filled the room again, until it stopped with a puff of steam. Relief sweeping over her, Evie rushed to the corner of the room, feeling for the Train's side. But before she reached it, the Captain came bursting out of the carriage door, panting and covered in dirt. He could barely stand. In fact, when he emerged from the Train, he practically collapsed into Evie's arms.

CHAPTER
19

EASY PREY

||||||||||||||||||||||||||||||||||||||||||||||||||||

Paulo and Silius were on Elisha's horse, travelling back towards the city of Jerusalem. Paulo admired Silius' horse-riding skills. He seemed to be able to command the horse effortlessly, without even falling off once! They could just see the hills surrounding Jerusalem ahead of them.

"What is a train?" said Silius.

Paulo smiled. "You're not going to believe me but here goes... it's a spaceship."

"What's a spaceship?"

"Oh, um..." Paulo was taken off guard. "A... mode of transport... that travels through space."

"Do not all modes of transport travel through space? That's what transport is."

"Good point. No, this one, um, travels in *outer* space. Among the stars and planets."

Silius was quiet for a moment, with a confused sort of smile. "That is not possible."

"Well, it also travels in time, and we're from the future and in the future, it *is* possible... I suppose."

Silius hesitated again, "...I had no idea."

Paulo smiled.

"I had no idea, that for the last two hours, I have been walking around with a lunatic."

"What? Well... where do you think this plant comes from then if not from another world?"

"All the Captain said was a little further away than another city. I do not..." he trailed off. They had heard a voice calling out.

"Hello! Stop please!"

Silius stopped the horse, and they saw a man running towards them. He was middle-age, with short black hair and beard, wearing Roman clothes. He was holding something that Paulo recognised.

"Are you alright?" asked Silius. "We are on our way to the city. Do you need help?"

The man panted. "I'm grateful to run into you." He squinted up at Silius, and when he glanced at Paulo, all the lines in his face flattened out. "*You.*"

Paulo frowned.

You've probably figured out that it was Marius,

having suddenly appeared in the wilderness. Still looking at Paulo, he asked Silius. "What I mean is... who is this with you? Is he a Jew?"

"Paulo is my friend," replied Silius.

"Paulo," Marius said softly, with hidden malice.

Paulo had been looking down at the device in Marius' hand, biting his lip. "May I ask," said Paulo, trying to sound casual, "how did you come by that strange looking object you have there?"

To Paulo's surprise, Marius replied in a more hushed and secretive voice, "It is a teleport device your friend lent to me to get you out of here. I'm sure you're familiar with it."

"What is a teleport device?" asked Silius.

"I don't understand it either," Marius said with apparent wonderment, "but your friend... the one you call... Captain? ...used it to send me out here to find you. I can take you right to him." Marius could tell Paulo wasn't pleased in the way he should have been. "What is troubling you?"

"Well it's not the Captain I'm worried about. I was hoping to find another friend of mine too. She was taken..."

"Is it Evie?" Marius interrupted, his face lighting up. "The Captain *found* Evie, they're together now."

"Really?"

"Yes! So there's no reason for you to hesitate."
He added, "They need your help!"

"For what? What's happening?"

"I do not know, I'm just passing on what he said." Marius grabbed the reins of the horse and led them the rest of the way into the city.

It was much better riding in the front of a wagon than it was riding in the back. Mostly because Evie wasn't alone anymore, and because the Captain gave her turns holding the reins.

After he'd tumbled out of the Train, Evie had noticed he was clutching a small glass bottle filled with a bright yellow syrupy liquid. He explained nothing, just said that they had to skedaddle. And after locking up the Train, he had asked Portia if they could borrow hers and Marius' wagon to skedaddle on. Portia, of course, asked question after question and with no time to explain, the Captain gave her a chance to skedaddle with them, but she chose to stay in the house and wait for Marius to return. She was so flustered and confused, she was hardly aware that her slave was skedaddling away in her own wagon. Anyway, Evie was now enjoying the ride and she chuckled to herself, thinking about her school friends, and if only they could see her now.

"Haven't you got questions whizzing around in your head?" the Captain said, breaking the silence.

"What, you want me to actually ask them?"

"Sure, go ahead."

"Okay, um... what's in the bottle? Where are we going? What's Kratilier Lumis? Where have you been? And what's that brown stuff on your face?"

"Let me see now... Yellow-venomed flat-top snake venom, around and about, a deadly plant, somewhere to *get* the yellow-venomed flat-top snake venom, and mud."

"What?"

"Alright it's not mud, it's Camazonian Bat poo, but they're very hygienic creatures so..."

"No I mean, what do you mean by *around and about*? We're not actually going anywhere?"

"Correct. We're looking for... ah ha." The Captain stopped mid-sentence when he'd spotted something. He stopped the wagon, jumped off and ran over to a nearby tree.

"Bat poo?" Evie said, hopping off after him. "Gross."

She found him crouching down in front of a small patch of dark purpley-green plant. He took a

165

cork stopper off the top of the bottle he was holding and then said with an air of hopefulness, "Here comes good old flat-top." He poured the tiniest drop of the bright yellow liquid onto the very edge of a small leaf growing out of the ground.

Before their very eyes, the leaves curled up at the edges and then shrivelled up. The effect grew, spreading out to the rest of the plant. In about seven seconds, the whole plant was clearly dead.

"Success," said the Captain, breathing relief.

"Okay," said Evie, staring at the ground. "Please explain."

The Captain put the cork back on the bottle and answered, "That was Kratilier Lumis. Otherwise known as Violet Assassin. The yellow-venomed flat-top snake lives in the same forest region as the plant. The ecosystem enables the plant to do its job for the surrounding wildlife, without growing out of control because of the presence of the snake. It's the only thing that can kill the plant apparently."

"That's amazing."

"Yes, amazing things like this are in every ecosystem. That's how ecosystems work."

"So you've just been..."

"Wrestling with a few yellow-venomed flat-top snakes, yes."

"But... how did the plant get here in the first place?"

"Have a think."

After a few seconds, Evie's brow uncreased. "Marius. He must have brought it with him – from wherever he's from. Where *is* he from?"

"That's not what's important now. What *is* important is that there's who-knows-how-many more patches of this stuff all over and surrounding Jerusalem. Perhaps even beyond."

"But how has it spread?"

"On people's shoes, horses, wagons."

"But it'd be everywhere!"

"Fortunately the Violet Assassin doesn't always take root. It's a difficult plant to get growing, especially in this dry heat."♣ He stood up and started walking back to the wagon.

"So we're literally just riding around looking for Violet Assassin to kill?"

"Quite literally, yes. But we do have to meet Paulo and another new friend of mine outside King Herod's palace at some stage. So we'd better get a wriggle on."

♣ For any budding gardeners out there, it needs partial sunlight and regular watering. It likes a moist environment with minimal drainage. Do not plant in your garden unless you also have a yellow-venomed flat-top snake.

Marius had led Paulo and Silius back into Jerusalem and to his own neighbourhood.

"My house is not much further," Marius panted and once they'd arrived, Portia came running out, demanding answers. All he said was "Not now, woman," and led Paulo and Silius straight down to his underground room. On the way, Marius quietly noticed that his horse and wagon were gone.

"This is where they were," said Marius breathlessly when they'd reached the bottom. "They were in this room, I don't understand."

"What did the Captain tell you?" said Paulo.

"He said he'd wait for us. They should be here... they must have been taken."

"Taken?"

"*Kidnapped!* They must be in terrible trouble."

"Kidnapped by whom?"*

"I don't know. The Captain spoke of some foreign character. Some person from another world he said, who was after his... train?"

"The *Train*?" cried Paulo. He was, if you're not already aware, stepping right into a trap.

---

* Paulo actually said 'who', but he should have said 'whom' so I took the liberty to change it.

"That's what he said. He also mentioned something about a... secret headquarters. Underneath er... the king's palace, where this person, or persons are hiding – making their plans."

"Could it be where they've taken Evie and the Captain?"

"I'd say that's a good guess."

"Well we should go there!" said Paulo. "Is it far? Do we have transport?"

"You would have a wagon of your own wouldn't you Marius?" said Silius.

"Yes... yes, *that's* how they must have got away. I noticed before that my wagon was gone!" Marius paced across the floor, and he 'deliberately-accidentally' walked into a large hard object... that no one could see. "What's this?"

When Paulo realised Marius was looking up at nothing, but convinced that something was there, his face lit up and he said, "Could it be? The Train!"

Marius was smiling inside. That silly girl Evie had done him a favour by bringing the Train back into existence. "Train, as in what the Captain spoke of?"

"Yes!" Paulo said, coming over and feeling the side of it with his hands. "We could use this..." then his enthusiasm dropped, "...if we knew how to operate it."

"Operate it? We have to get *into* the thing first," Marius said.

"I don't understand," said Silius. "I don't see anything!"♣

"This is the Captain's spaceship I was telling you about. Feel." Paulo put Silius' hand out so that it touched the smooth metal panelling. Then he needed no more encouragement from Marius. He reached into one of his overall pockets and pulled out a long thin wiry object. "If I can just get inside, I might be able to figure out how to drive it. Setting the coordinates for our destination shouldn't be too hard. I've seen the Captain do it once." Paulo was poking at the space with the small object, twisting it around and jiggling it back and forth. It was a lock-pick. One of Paulo's up-until-now hidden talents.

As Marius patiently watched and waited, Paulo manipulated the lock with his pick, starting to think that the Captain would have been cleverer than to put a lock on his Train that could be picked open. But soon, there was a click and then a door-openingy sound. (It was a very good lock pick.) Paulo could see the interior of the Train. He walked in and was followed by one baffled Roman, and

---

♣ Of course, if Paulo stopped and thought for a second or two, he would have realised that this is what Marius should have been saying too.

another pretending-to-be-baffled pretend-Roman.

Paulo and Marius hopped up on board, but Marius stopped Silius from following. "Perhaps you should stay here. In case anyone comes back." Silius agreed. Marius grinned with dark glee as he followed Paulo into the engine room.

CHAPTER

WANNA BET?

"So what exactly are we fighting here?" asked Evie as they destroyed a second patch of Violet Assassin. "The plant? Marius?"

"The plant is merely a symptom of the greater problem," the Captain replied. "I believe it's Marius who is the problem."

"What does he want?"

"It would seem that he wants the Train."

"Is that it? Not world domination. Not to take over people's minds?"

"Certainly not. I think all he wants to do is get away from them."

"He said he wanted his life back. If he had transport..."

"We're talking *intergalactic* transport."

"...Then he'd be happy and leave everyone alone?"

"Well..."

"He could just hitch a ride with us."

"Mmm..."

"I mean, he creeps me out and he may or may not be a killer... but you're into being kind to your enemies aren't you?"

"I'm not sure it'll be as simple as that. He probably wants what I can't give him. Freedom to travel wherever and *when*ever he wants."

"He might not."

"He might not. But I'd be prepared to put my money on it."

"How much?"

"No, I don't actually want to bet. It's a figure of speech. Let's go, we've got a lot to do."

As they were climbing back onto the wagon, Evie said, "What's that huge building over there?"

The Captain looked up. "That's the Temple. Don't you look at the illustrations at the back of your Bible?"

"The actual Temple of Jerusalem?"

"Yep."

"Can we go there?"

"Don't see why not. There might be some

173

Violet Assassin growing there. Come on."

The engine room of the Train rattled and the sound of the steam building up filled their ears. Paulo was smiling and, in the shadows, in the corner of the room, Marius was smiling too.

"That's got it started," Paulo said. "Not quite as smooth as when the Captain does it, but I thought it would be harder to be honest. Now, how can I find a map of this city?" he said to himself.

Marius could see the keyboard and monitor. He came over, examined the control panel for a moment, and then started pressing buttons.

"What are you doing?" said Paulo.

"I'm looking up the coordinates for the palace, of course."

"How do you know how to do that?"

Marius didn't say anything. Paulo stepped over. "That's not Jerusalem," Paulo realised. "That's... that's not even Earth. What are you doing?" He grabbed Marius' arm but Marius knocked him back.

"Who are you really?" said Paulo.

Marius sniggered. He figured out how to lock in coordinates and then turned to face Paulo. He'd dropped the Roman accent. Now it was similar to the Captain's English accent. "Thanks to you, you gullible, lock-picking, overalled, air-head, I finally have my freedom. My *salvation!*" Then he laughed. "It's so hilariously ironic that it's *you* who did it. Like you're making it up to me. *Apologising...*" he came close to Paulo's face and sneered angrily, "for imprisoning me here in the first place."

"*Me?* What do you..."

"And when I learn how to fly this thing, I certainly won't be needing you anymore."

"But... what about the Captain and Evie?" Paulo said, trying to understand. "And your wife?"

Marius' gaze dropped for a moment, before he replied, "My life here was no more than a disguise. A temporary affliction. But now it's over. And not you, nor the Captain, nor my so-called once-leader *Mortimer Murdock* can stop me!" He pulled a lever and the Train bounded into action.

"Hullo, what's this?" said the Captain when they had almost reached the temple. They'd had to stop nearby, where a construction project appeared to be underway.

"What?" said Evie.

The Captain pulled out the beeping Unique Radio-Wave-Operated Link Chip from his pocket. "Someone's using the Train."

"How can that be?" she asked, worriedly. "You have the only key, right?"

"Perhaps I shouldn't have left it there unattended."

"I think *definitely* you shouldn't have left it..."

"Wait a second, wait a second, don't panic. Whoever's driving won't get far, look, I can do something specky. Watch." He turned a tiny dial on the device and waved it around up in the air like you would if you were trying to get mobile reception.

At that moment, there was another big **THUD!** in the engine room of the Train. Marius was being told by the controls that the time-and-space travelling vessel was materialising.

"No!" Marius growled at Paulo, pulling his gun out. "What have you done?"

"I haven't done anything. I promise."

*

The Captain put the Link-Chip away, hopped out of the wagon and put on his Train-driving goggles. Evie watched him walk boldly away, and suddenly, Paulo stepped out of thin air nearby. Evie was happy and relieved for one and a half seconds, but then

Marius stepped out after him. And he was discreetly holding his pistol to Paulo's back.

The Captain's face was a stone wall. Only *he* knew what unsettling fears were hiding behind it.

"Ah! Captain, *finally!*" said Marius.

"Where is Silius, Paulo?" the Captain said carefully and calmly.

"It's alright, he stayed behind," Paulo said stiffly.

The Captain breathed out quietly with relief.

"Yes, it's lucky I still have this one," Marius said, giving Paulo a shove. "Perhaps as a bargaining chip."

"I don't like gambling," said the Captain.

Marius smiled. "Then simply allow me to take off and no one will be hurt."

Ignoring this, the Captain said, "What's your real name? 'Marius' is so uncannily Roman and you're clearly not. I'd like to know who I'm going to be handing my Train over to."

"It's Mallory. *Great Cup,* it's strange you not knowing me yet."

"Why do you want the Train?"

"I've wasted over eight years of my life being stuck here. I just want to leave this place."

"Why can't you leave the way you came?"

Mallory gave a short bitter chuckle. "If only it was that easy. This *boy*," he nudged Paulo in the

177

back with his gun, "...I was sent here. Against my will. And then I was abandoned by your... I once called him partner. My *beloved* leader. He managed to escape, but his device could only take one person. We only had a few minimal resources. And what he left me was even more meagre. I tried to create another teleporter, but I ended up creating something... quite different. When it finally detected something useful in the space-time vortex, I seized the opportunity. I didn't know it was *you*.

"Anyway because my *creation* can't teleport people, there was no way I could find my own salvation in it. But it could bring my salvation to me."

"At a cost. Who was this partner of yours?"

"I'm surprised you haven't worked it out. You at least know where I'm from don't you?"

The Captain nodded nervously.

"Don't worry. It's not you I'm after. Are you giving me the Train or not?"

"Don't Captain," cried Paulo, and Marius tightened his grip on him.

"Would you accept a lift somewhere?"

"I want permanent transport, Captain Dumbo. I can't just go home; I'd be a prisoner. I'm going to finally be my own boss, with the freedom to travel anywhere, any time. Just like you apparently have."

The Captain turned around to Evie. "There, I asked for you."

"Well sometimes we don't always get what we want!" shouted Evie. "That's life!"

The Captain, still looking at her, raised his eyebrows in surprise. He was almost proud. But he told her softly, "Usually men with guns at your friend's back tend to get what they want, Evelyn."

Evie shut her mouth, now content to stay quiet.

"Well?" Mallory shouted, with growing impatience. "Captain... *Murdock.*"

"My name's not Murdock," the Captain replied calmly but with a dark edge. "This Train swap thing... What's in it for me?"

Evie and Paulo panicked.

"Your friend doesn't die."

"I want more in return. That's not just transport to me, it's my home. So I'll expect my teleport device back for one."

"What, this?" Mallory pulled it out of his pocket, smiling mockingly. "Alright, if you wish. It's not much use anyway. Short-range and primitive. But I won't give it to you until I have your guarantee I can fly away in this thing."

"Captain, what are you doing?" said Evie.

"Life is awfully short," the Captain told her, then he turned back to Mallory, "and there isn't time for fighting and fussing. It's a deal."

"Captain, no!" yelled Paulo.

"Wise choice," said Mallory, not giving up the teleport device just yet. He looked around. "This is quite a convenient spot, Captain. See that cistern?"

The Captain had been aware that it was there.[*] "Yes," he replied calmly.

"That's where you're going. You and your little crew."

"Oh I don't think that's necessary," said the Captain with a smile, as though all he was doing was humbly rejecting a 'thankyou' gift.

"Oh I think it is. I don't trust you to just let me disappear. I know you."

The Captain narrowed his eyes. "I figured that."

"You'd probably have another trick up your sleeve. So to make sure this time," he held up his hand that wasn't holding the gun and revealed some metal chains. "Move," he said.

"Come along Evelyn," said the Captain.

Evie joined him. Mallory, with the gun constantly at Paulo's back, forced them all to approach the old, crumbling cistern. The ground

---

[*] A cistern, as you and I know it, is the little tank of water that sits above the toilet seat. But in ancient times, it was a large concrete tank beneath the ground to supply water to a community – for bathing, washing, sometimes drinking. This one was very old and wasn't being used anymore. The ground had been dug up around it, revealing the opening.

was rocky and uneven, dusty pebbles rolled under foot. Just inside the entrance, there was a sharp decline. The air was musty, moldy and stifled. Inky blackness lurked beyond. All Evie wanted to do was get out.

Mallory quickly bound them up to the wall of the cistern. Luckily for him there were built-in 'safety' handles, put there so that in case anyone ever got trapped in the cistern, they would be able to hold themselves above the water until someone realised they were down there. What was intended as a safety precaution, was to become their doom.

Soon, they were trapped. Evie closest to the entrance, then Paulo, then the Captain. All in a row.

"And I suppose this is how you recalled the Train back into time and space just then eh, Captain?" Mallory said, confiscating the Link-Chip. "We can't have you keeping that now, can we?" He dropped it on the ground right in front of the Captain and stomped his heel down hard on it, crushing it to pieces against the rocky cistern floor. "Well, I best be on my way. I bet they're going to fill this old cistern in so that they can build on it. Probably why they've got all that cement up there, ready to use. When the time comes, give my past-self my regards."

"But you've got what you wanted," growled

Paulo. "Why trap us in here?"

"I told you. So that you don't try anything clever while I take off. And..." his eyes bore into Paulo's, "...perhaps I have my own scores to settle."

"What's to stop us from calling out for someone to rescue us?" said Evie.

"Mmm," he said in mock thought. "Perhaps this." He pulled out a cloth from his pocket and covered the crew's faces one by one, forcing them to breathe in whatever the cloth had been soaked in. They couldn't do anything to stop him, and within a few seconds, they all fell asleep. Mallory stepped back and looked at them, putting the cloth back in his pocket. "Happy dreams," he said and climbed back up the crumbling slope out of sight.

While the three of them hung there sleeping, there was a **Chuff**CHOOFETY *chuffing* that slowly faded out of space and time.

CHAPTER

POCKETS

Mum came into Evie's bedroom with a bowl of hot water and suds. This was the good part about being sick. Being taken care of by mum. She slid her feet down blissfully into the bowl and melted into it, restful, warm, loved. But the water grew cold as soon as her mum left the room. Evie watched her walking further and further away down a never-ending hallway, the image of her fading slowly into a distant foggy blackness. Her feet were freezing. She tried lifting them out of the bowl but the water had thickened and started sticking to her. It formed vein-like roots that climbed up her legs. When she tried to stand, she found the roots had taken hold of her calves and they began to pull her down. She tried to call out. Her voice wouldn't come...

She jerked awake. It took her a few moments to remember where she was. She looked down at her feet and with the little light there was, saw that they were indeed completely covered by muck. A cold and sticky mixture that looked like rocky mud, bits of straw and goodness knows what else. There was a churning sound of wood grating against stone. Beside her was Paulo, and beside *him*, the Captain – both still fast asleep. With all the body movement she could manage, she nudged Paulo and yelled as best as she could in his ear.

He woke up slowly, blinking his eyes, and then went through the same moment of panic as Evie had a moment ago.

"Wake up the Captain," Evie said. "We've got to get out of here!"

"What happened?" said Paulo.

"I don't know. We fell asleep somehow and now they've started filling in this hole."

"Marius must be miles away by now."

"Lightyears, more like."

"What are we going to do without the Train?"

"I don't know. But one thing I *do* know is that the Captain's gone mad. He practically handed the Train over to him gift-wrapped."

"And now we're going to be drowned in this...

what is this stuff anyway?"

"Cement. The ancient formula. You know, the old quicklime, pozzolana and pumice." It wasn't Evie's voice.

"Captain! You're awake," said Evie.

"Yes. And I heard you use the 'm' word when referring to me."

"What, *mad?* Well you are!"

"No need for flattery. What seems to be the trouble?"

"What seems to be the trouble?" said Evie. "We're going to be buried alive. That's what the trouble is!"

"Yes, I'll admit it's quite a sticky situation."

"Are you trying to be funny?"

"Though I must say, it's quite interesting too."

"Interesting?"

"To actually witness the building methods of biblical times. I'd say they're using some sort of gutter-like structure to pour in the cement. They were clever back in these times, you know. They managed quite a lot without computers and machines and robots. Mind you, they did have to work harder. It would be good to get out there and see it in action."

"Yes! That would be great!" said Evie. How had she ever managed to trust the Captain? She called

185

out as loud as she could, "HELP!!!"

Paulo joined her. "HELP!!!!!"

No one appeared to hear them. All that happened was this: the end of a gutter-like structure appeared at the opening of the cistern and down it, sludged a thick, gluggy stream of cement. The three prisoners could feel the cold, wet substance forming a new surface level around their calves.

"This underground hole absorbs a lot of sound," said the Captain. "And most of the builders could actually be some distance away..."

"And what about the Train," Evie said, showing a hint of her anger.

"Ah yes, well I was going to explain about that, you see..."

Another load of cement came slopping down into the hole.

"Never mind explaining now," said Paulo. "We should concentrate on getting out of here first."

"First thing," the Captain said, "keep your legs moving. This cement won't set as quickly as modern cement, but best keep it moving anyhow."

"Is there a second thing?" said Evie.

"Yes. Turn out your pockets."

Paulo went to do so but... "We can't, our hands are tied up."

"Oh yes. Well, try and remember what's in

your pockets and we'll decide if any of it's useful. Evelyn?"

"Um... a hair tie I think, and... there'd be that tissue I used the other day."

"O...kay, not a good start. Paulo?"

"My lock pick that I used to open the Train..."

"I should confiscate that, you rascal." He sighed, "But it's a pity these aren't handcuffs instead of chains. Pick the locks, away we go. Go on."

"Er... I have a small spanner and a screwdriver. And some figs."

"Oooh," said the Captain, giving the others a glimpse of hope.

"You reckon the acidity of the fruit could corrode the chains or something?"

"No, I reckon we could eat them. I'm starving, aren't you? Anything else?"

"Not that I can think of," said Paulo. "What have you got Captain?"

"Yeah, you seem to carry a whole hardware and electronics store around in your pockets," said Evie. "You must have something good."

"Now let me see... my glasses and Train goggles. The flat-top snake venom, my Portable Audio Clandestine Digital Communicators,[*] my Manual

---

[*] In other words, a pair of walky-talkies.

Hand Operating Fuel Injected... sorry, my *lighter*. The Atom Relocating Molecular Teleport Device if Mallory kept his word, my Vernacular Recognition and Decoding Box,♦ a handkerchief, and that's all I can remember. Unfortunately, the Link Chip is crushed to bits somewhere under all this muck."

"So anything useful out of all that?" Evie asked.

"Not really. Just the teleport, but it's recharging. You sure you don't still have that whistle on you Evelyn?"♠

"No, I left it on the Train," she replied, realising how annoyingly brilliant it would be if she still had it.

"So what are we going to do?" said Paulo.

Another load of cement came slurping down and sloshing uncomfortably around their knees.

"Captain?" Evie said urgently.

The Captain was glad Evie and Paulo couldn't see the uncertainty on his own face in the poor light. Even if he could come up with an impressive plan to escape using the objects in their pockets, he first needed an impressive plan to get *into* their pockets. He tried tugging fiercely at the chains, quickly becoming tired. What he didn't he know, was that

---

♦ Possibly an explanation as to why Roman and Jewish people seem to have been speaking English.

♠ A whistle that had saved quite a number of lives on their last adventure.

the brittle wall behind him was weakening, just beginning to lose its grip on the iron handles...

The cement reached their hips. Every muscle in their legs was burning from marching them through the thick substance. Evie had a horrible feeling, as the sludge climbed up to her tummy, that she'd be marching like this for the rest of her life.

CHAPTER

COMMOTION AT THE INN

At an inn near the center of Jerusalem, wealthy guests reclined on carpets and cushions and sipped at wine with their jewelled fingers as they laughed and conversed. But a commotion of horse hooves clopping loudly on the ground outside broke out suddenly and dust was kicked up in clouds all around. An exhausted, dishevelled woman fell from the horse and picked her way through the busy street outside the inn. She stumbled through the crowds, and when they caught glimpse of her, they screamed and gasped in horror.

"Get away from me!"

"Leper!"

"Don't let her touch you!"

When she came to the entrance of the inn and reached out with her discoloured arm, the inn-keeper rushed to the door, stood against it and said, "We're full up here, sorry!"

The woman had already wedged her foot in the door and was leaning against it.

"Please woman, I have nowhere for you here!"

"Please, I need help!" she said desperately.

"There's nothing I can do for you." The innkeeper had heard the l-word.♣ He wasn't going to risk his life, let alone his business. His guests had started to notice the commotion and were coming to watch from a safe distance.

"I can't let you in here," the inn-keeper persisted. "You *should not* be here!"

"This is not leprosy," she tried to tell him. "Please, I need help."

"But there is no physician here to..."

"Portia?" He was interrupted by a voice behind him. The person pushed his way through the curious, disgusted onlookers and came up beside the inn-keeper. "It is you, Portia!" The man went to open the door, but the inn-keeper insisted on

♣ Leprosy, you must understand, is a highly contagious skin disease and in bible times, you'd most likely die from it. If you had leprosy, you weren't allowed to come near others, unless of course, they also happened to already have leprosy. Then you could live together in leprousness.

keeping it closed.

Portia knew him. Lucius, her brother-in-law.

"What's happened Portia?"

"I do not know," she coughed. "But I think I am dying."

Cassia came up beside Lucius. "Oh dear, Portia. For pity's sake, man, let her in," she said to the inn-keeper.

"If I do, I place everyone here – including myself – in great danger."

Cassia broke past the man, and her and Lucius went outside the inn and shut the door behind them.

"This is not leprosy," repeated Portia.

"Any fool can see that. But what is it?"

"I... think it's poison. Something's wrong in my throat. And look at my skin!"

"We must call on Cardea..." said Lucius.

"Calling for your goddess of health is no good," came a new voice from around the side of the inn.

"Levi, how dare you scoff the gods," said Cassia. "Why is it do you think they do not choose to honour you."

"The God I believe in is the God of health, land, sky, water, light, everything."

"Do you know what is wrong with Portia?"

"No, I have never seen anything like this."

"Well then do not speak."

"We could take her to the temple for prayer," Levi said.

The pair almost told him off for speaking so boldly, but Portia was family. They were willing to try anything, and they had no time to lose. Lucius said, "His God is as good as any, come on."

The inn-keeper shouted from his window, "You haven't paid yet!"

Lucius looked at Levi. "Levi, *you* must take Portia to the temple and have her prayed for. Do all you can, do you understand?"

"Yes."

"And return as soon as you can to bring news."

"Yes, of course." Levi blasted into action, sitting Portia in their wagon, untroubled by her sickness. He pounded the horse off along the road, towards the great Temple of Jerusalem.

When they finally got there, Levi had to stop the wagon short. A Judean soldier was blocking the way and behind him was a big busy mess of workers, building equipment, piles of dirt, mud and straw, and all sorts of digging and building tools.

"Where do you want to go?" asked the solider.

"The temple. It is very urgent!"

"You have to go around. Can you not see there is building in progress? By order of King Herod."

Levi breathed through flared, impatient nostrils, but he hurriedly got the horse moving again. He heard a grunt from Portia, followed by a choking sound. "Stay awake Mistress, don't give up! We're nearly there!"

CHAPTER

THE LETHAL LAKE

The cement was quickly reaching the Captain's ribcage. Because Paulo was a little shorter than him, it was settling around his chest. And because Evie was the shortest of them all, the cement was swirling around her shoulders!

Evie could not hold back her panicking tears. "Captain *do* something! I'm scared!" In fact she had never been so scared in her life.

If the Captain was scared too, he had a funny way of showing it. He let out a sudden, confident, and slightly hysterical laugh. "Don't you see what this means? No way at all of getting out of here?"

"Yes, it means we'll die!"

"No! No no no no no! I only want positive

thinking, thank you."

"Sorry, Captain but I can't think of anything positive at the moment."

"We have no way of escape, we're absolutely helpless, which means if we get out of this situation, which we will, it'll be a full-sized, no-doubt, utterly pure miracle! It'll make a fantastic story to tell!"

"But... that's *if* we get out. Aren't you scared?"

The Captain breathed in and out deeply, and then a gleam came to his eye. *What do You have planned I wonder?*

Evie wished she had the Captain's faith. Sure, she believed in God. But miracles like what the Captain was expecting, only happened in Bible times. Things like Moses parting the Red Sea, Jesus feeding thousands of people from just five loaves of bread and two fish. Or was it five fish and two loaves of bread? She could never remember which way round it was.

But suddenly, she remembered two things. She was *in* Bible times. Perhaps a miracle *would* happen. And she also remembered the strange unexplained 'miracle-like' thing that had happened last time the three of them were in a tricky situation.

She kept hoping and praying. She wriggled her hands in the chains behind her back. The cement was thickening, gluing itself to the chains and to the wall behind her. Her breaths became short and fast; she could not control it. She wondered if this was what a panic attack was like. She cried out as loud as she could, but choked on her tears.

"Stay calm, Evelyn," said the Captain. "Everything's going to be alright."

"That's easier for you to say, you're only in up to your chest!"

"Keep pulling at the chains. They might give."

"I think my chains are cemented to the wall, Captain," said Paulo. He felt it crawling up past his shoulders and Evie cried out again when she felt it touch her chin.

These are my last moments, she thought. *Mum'll never know what happened to me. Dad'll probably talk about that time I spilt milk all over him at my funeral to try and lighten the mood. And James… James'll think I died way back on Satellite SB-1:7.*

The Captain tried again, pulling at the chains and this time… "Arghh! My hands are free! I did it!"

"Quick get us out!" Evie exploded.

The Captain took a step towards his friends as quickly as he could, which was extremely slow, given the thickness of the liquid slowly turning into a solid.

But when his foot landed on the ground beneath him, it slid with an unexpected jerk and his leg gave way underneath him. His head disappeared beneath and surface. Evie screamed in terror.

"Captain!" Paulo called, still yanking on his own chains.

There was movement under the surface and the Captain's head emerged again – unrecognisable. He wiped away the cement from his mouth and eyes and waded carefully over to Evie. She was the priority, since she was about to be submerged.

He reached his arms above her head where her hands were bound. He noticed her legs weren't moving anymore. "Evelyn, keep moving," he said calmly in her ear.

"I can't. When I move, it goes in my mouth."

There was no time to waste. Soon there would be another load of cement sloshing down the gutter, and that would be the load that smothered her.

Evie whimpered, "Get them undone, please Captain. I want to get out of here."

The Captain couldn't bear hearing Evie's voice so frightened. It was because of him that she and Paulo were here. He was responsible for them both. While his fingers felt the knot of chains, his stomach felt a burning hot stirring as impatience welled up.

Evie could hear him muttering under his

breath, but she couldn't understand the words. But then all of a sudden, she recognised a name.

"Jesus..."

The chains felt loose, as though, like a bullet, the name had blasted them apart.

"Now Paulo," said the Captain. And at that very moment, they could hear another load rolling down the gutter and slopping down into what was now an underground, cement lake.

"No!" the Captain yelled, just as he saw both Paulo and Evie taking a deep breath, preparing to go under. "Evie, get out! We'll be right behind you!"

But there was no chance of leaving. And not because she was having a jolly time. She could find no foothold, nothing to get a grip on to heave herself out to safety. Every time she took a step, the ground was deeper than she expected, and her body plummeted forward, leaving her arms thrashing around. It was like every time she took a step forward, a force was dragging her back.

"I can't get out!" she cried.

"I can't loosen Paulo's chains!" the Captain replied.

"Hello?!!" Another voice cried... "Is someone down there?"

Evie couldn't believe it. "Yes!!" she screamed. "Yes! Down here!" She couldn't see anything; just heard running footsteps.

"What happened?" said a young man's voice.

"Just help us, please! There's three of us!"

Whoever he was, he wasn't afraid of getting dirty. Not realising Evie's own struggle to get out, he headed straight for the Captain, whom he could see was trying to get a third person free.

The Captain briefed the newcomer, "I'm trying to get the chains undone. It's what's holding him to the wall."

"I'll do that, you keep his head above the surface."

The Captain held his hand under Paulo's chin.

Evie had found the wall and was trying to walk along it, but another load had been dropped in and she couldn't touch the bottom. *Splosh!* She lost her footing and was now buried under the surface. She flapped her arms and legs like a person insane, but it was useless. No amount of pushing or paddling got her anywhere near the surface again.

It was somebody's hand that grabbed her arm. She was dragged slowly through the cement and soon, she could feel coolness on her face, could breathe through her open mouth again, and then, she could walk. She was out!

"Got it!" the boy said suddenly from back within the cistern. The Captain started dragging

Paulo towards the entrance. The boy helped to push him along but stumbled, as he was no taller than Paulo. The Captain had to pull both of them along.

Evie had landed on the person who had pulled her out. She wiped the cement away from her eyes. "Portia!"

Portia herself could not speak. She just curled over, weak and frail, and coughed and coughed and coughed into the ground.

"What's wrong?"

The three others were crawling out of the pit. They looked like horrible undead monsters rising up out of a stagnant, sludgy swamp. When the boy spoke, Evie realised it was Levi. *What a miracle!* she couldn't help thinking.

"Portia needs help too," Levi said, breathlessly. "She can't breathe properly, and her skin is changing. I was on my way to the temple to pray for her."

"Sounds like the state Silius was in," said the Captain, also short of breath. "Did you come into contact with any strange plants?" he asked Portia.

"In Marius' stable," Portia wheezed. "There was a crateful of some plant I've never seen before."

The Captain turned to Paulo. "Do you still have

201

that fig in your pocket?"

"Yes!" Paulo said, hoping it wasn't squashed to a pulp. He pulled it out, and because his sky-blue overall pockets had zips, the fruit was unharmed. He gave it to Portia. "Here! Eat this, quick!"

CHAPTER

GATE BEAUTIFUL

Levi still planned to go to the temple and it wasn't for the Captain to argue. An opportunity to see the famous Temple of Jerusalem in its glory was too good to miss. When the five of them approached, they *would* have looked like tourists gazing up at it in the late afternoon sun, only they were covered in cement. So instead, they looked more like rock monsters.

The place was bustling with activity. There were people everywhere. Walking, queuing, buying, selling. There was clinking of coins, calves grunting, lambs bleating, doves cooing. There were men walking around dressed in long black and white robes. These were the priests and religious leaders.

Some of them were taking the animals from the queued people, and some were in groups having loud conversations. It was a noisy, crowded, lively, joyous, smokey and smelly place.

The spacious courtyard was paved with colourful cobble stone and Levi was heading straight through to a big, beautiful, decorative gate.♣ As he was about to go in, he turned back and said politely to the Captain, Paulo and Evie, "You cannot come any further. I don't think you are Jewish, are you?"

The three looked at each other. The Captain answered. "Well no, we're not."

Then Levi looked at Portia. "I will go on ahead and pray on your behalf."

"But why should your God extend his protection over me – a Roman?"

"My God is a God of mercy and His mercy is not limited to one people. Have you heard the stories about Rahab and Ruth? They were ancestors of King David, yet they were not Israelites. God gave *them* mercy. And many more."

"I have not heard," sighed Portia, sounding like she had pebbles in her throat. "But if there is such a God as merciful as yours, I want to know Him."

Levi gave all of them a polite smile and

♣ Believe it or not, the gate was actually called 'Gate Beautiful'.

continued on through the temple.

"Can't Portia even go any further in?" Evie asked the Captain. "She's the sick one."

"It's not a hospital." The Captain went on to explain that this courtyard where they were standing was the 'Court of the Gentiles'. If you weren't a Jew, you were called a Gentile and were permitted to come this far. "The next chamber," he went on, "is called the 'Court of Women'. Levi could take her there if she was Jewish."

"Does the 'Court of Women' mean that *women* aren't allowed to go any further?" Evie asked.

"Yes," said the Captain. When he saw Evie was about to protest, he added, "This is a very different world from yours. Women were generally seen as lower than men, socially."

"But Christians don't think that."

"It's the culture and the time, not Christianity. Not that Christians even exist yet. And Jesus certainly didn't agree with everything *culture* says."

"Captain, I know you probably haven't forgotten," said Paulo, quietly, so that Portia couldn't hear, "but after all this, we still don't have the Train. You act as though everything's okay, but Mallory could be anywhere in the entire universe by now. What are we going to do?"

"Or is this our new home now, Captain?" said

205

Evie, trying to stay patient with him.

All the Captain did was raise his eyebrows as if he'd just remembered something exciting.

Portia was gaining strength on the journey back to her house. The Captain wanted to collect Elisha's horse which Paulo said was still there. They yoked him to the wagon with the other horse and then travelled back to the inn. There they all got to have a good wash in the inn's bathing pool and the innkeeper kindly lent them some clothes while their own clothes dried in the sun.

The Captain tried to explain all he could to Portia. "From what I can gather, Marius was stranded here by a former accomplice. He wasn't from this world, so he had to learn this culture fast. He met you... he may have fallen in love, but... well he did need to blend in. And as soon as he had the chance to escape, he took it. I'm sorry."

"Without even saying goodbye," said Evie, feeling sad for Portia. "You'll be alright, won't you?"

"I do not know," she said, her eyes desolate. "I have my sister. And Lucius."

"And me," said Levi, shrugging.

"Dear Levi," Portia said, laying a hand on his

shoulder. "I owe you my life. Thank your God for me. He is yet another god of health that must be remembered."

Levi politely smiled. It wasn't his place to talk about faith with his masters.

Then, Portia persisted. "Will you teach me? About your God?"

Levi's eyes looked back into hers earnestly, and he gave one polite nod of the head. "As you wish."

"Well, we must be on our way," said the Captain, grabbing hold of the reins on Elisha's trusty horse. He gestured to Paulo and Evie to hop on.

"Three people can't fit on there!" said Evie.

"Who says? You can do it, can't you old boy!" he said, patting the horse's neck. It bobbed its head and let out a short snort of air from its wide nostrils. The Captain took that as a yes. "Yes, you're a good boy, aren't you! I'm going to call you Henry."

"Henry?"

"Anyway, it won't be for long. We'll pick up Elisha's other horse from the palace along the way."

"On our way where?"

There was no answer from the Captain yet. Before he mounted the horse, however, he reached into his pocket and pulled out the bottle of thick, bright yellow fluid. "Levi, there's something important I need you to do. And you'll need help."

He explained about the Violet Assassin.

Levi still had lots of questions. (So did Evie and Paulo for that matter!) He said, "I would do as you say, only I am not free to make my own decisions."

Portia butted in, "I will do this thing with Levi. No one should suffer what I suffered." She took the bottle from him. "You say just one small drop?"

"A *tiny* drop. It should affect any bits of plant that are connected to the same root system."

"You can rely on us Captain," said Levi.

With Levi's help, Paulo got up on the horse behind the Captain, and Evie squeezed on behind Paulo, feeling very unstable.

"Thank you for saving our lives!" the Captain said to Levi and Portia. "And God be with you." He winked and then commanded the horse to get a move on. "Valeo!"

Henry the horse took off with a loud neigh.

"Faster, faster!" shouted the Captain, like a little child getting a piggy-back ride on his dad.

"Slower, slower!" cried Evie.

"Sorry Evelyn, you're going to have to hold on!"

And with that, they accelerated even more.

CHAPTER

BREAKING FREE

Two horses were now galloping south, side by side across the wide-open hills and plains of Judea. Henry and Henderson, (as the Captain had named them) charged on majestically, their hooves pounding into the earth, their robust form working with such grace and magnificence, and their manes rippling elegantly.

Paulo was now riding the other horse, Henderson. The Captain was riding Henry, with Evie holding on for dear life behind him, her body buzzing with excitement and adrenalin. Her lungs were gasping for air. Even though she was breathing in so much of it, it never seemed to be enough. And even though it was terrifying, she was smiling. It was that exhilarating mix of terror and fear, joy and ecstasy and it's like your face isn't sure what to do.

"Where are we going?!" Evie shouted in his ear above the hiss of the wind racing past.

"We're going back to where it all started!" the Captain called over his shoulder. "We're going to get the Train back!"

They didn't know whether this was a simple statement, or hopeful, positive thinking. Whatever it was, it filled them with hope too.

After a long ride across open, grassy fields, the Captain began to slow his horse down.

"What are we doing?" said Evie.

"Looking for the Train!"

She was confused. "Train *tracks?*"

"No, the *Train*. Don't you want to go home one day?"

"But..." said Evie.

"Are you okay, Captain?" said Paulo.

"Never felt better! As long as my lock's worked properly."

"What lock?"

"When Mallory was talking to us outside the temple, I put a lock on the Train's controls..."

Evie breathed relief. "Why didn't you say so?"

"Don't count your chickens yet," he said quickly. "There's a few things that could go wrong.

The link chip I used to activate the lock got destroyed and would be half-set in cement underneath Jerusalem by now, so it's possible the lock was disabled. It could also just simply not work properly. *And*, it might be possible to 'pick the lock' in a manner of speaking." He tossed a glance to Paulo.

Paulo felt his stomach twist.

"What sort of lock?" Evie asked from behind.

"When activated, the Train can only jump to a pre-specified area. I specified here. It seemed the safest place. Well out of the way." The Captain then slowed Henry down to a gentle walk to where the Train had landed three nights ago. That historic night. The birth of salvation. He had not known then, that his landing there, was the birth of someone else's salvation. Or at least the attempt.

When the horse stopped, every muscle in Evie's body relaxed. Even her head flopped down onto the Captain's back. Then Henderson raced past with Paulo holding on for dear life. "Captain!"

"Pull on the reins, Paulo!" called the Captain, getting out his train-driving goggles. He handed them back to Evie. "Here, put these on."

She lifted her head wearily and put them on.

211

The Captain got out the pair of glasses that also had the special lenses in them, and slid them onto his face.

"I can't see it," Evie said. "What do we do if it's not here?"

"We just... pray that it *is* here."

Paulo was just trotting Henderson back to them. "To your Friend? Our *Maker* on Serothia? But, *you're* saying He's a *baby* here. I'm not sure this is the same *Friend* after all. What can a baby do?"

"Well *God* isn't a baby... sort of." Evie put in. She had a vague understanding that Jesus and God were the same person.

"It's the same Friend," the Captain told Paulo. "My theory is that Serothians are the ones who are different. And because of that, I don't think God ever became a baby on your world."

"Never became a baby?" Evie said with growing interest.

"He didn't need to. Think about how Serothians are all so peaceful and don't know about things like hatred and violence and lying. They don't even know the concept of guilt."

"I don't understand," said Paulo.

"This world... as I'm sure you've figured out by now," the Captain told Paulo, "...is a bit messed up."

"Yes I did notice," said Paulo, thinking about

the Roman soldiers' orders, the dungeon and the weapons... "It's a bit different from Serothia."

"Your people... never rebelled. And so never experienced shame and the need to cover up mistakes. Never needed forgiveness. You've always been in perfect step with each other and with your Maker. You didn't need rescuing from yourselves. Like we do."

Evie cut in, "So you're saying... Jesus didn't have to..." Her voice trailed off at that moment. They'd approached the crest of another hill and the Captain had stopped the horse. "I can't believe it," she said softly.

Paulo didn't know what they had seen, but a wide grin spread all over the Captain's face like runny honey on hot toast. "Yes," he said calmly and trotted Henry down the hillside.

Paulo clumsily took off after him and when they came to another stop, Evie leant over and passed Paulo the goggles.

The Captain dismounted, giving Henry a generous pat on the neck. He then took out a key from one of his pockets and opened the carriage door. When the other two reached his side, he turned and stopped them. "Wait here." Stepping up into the carriage room of his Train, he saw Mallory slumped on one of the sofas, looking weak, pale and exhausted.

"I have some almond biscuits you could have helped yourself to," is all the Captain said.

Mallory didn't move. His eyes rolled upwards to look at the Captain. "You took your time getting here," he croaked out of a slit in his bearded mouth.

"Sorry. I would have gotten here sooner, only some lunatic chained my friends and me down in a cistern leaving us to be buried alive in cement. Can you believe that?" He shrugged and shook his head with a *'tut'* of his tongue.

Mallory's eyes closed. He frowned as if in pain. "Water," he rasped.

The Captain raced into the engine room and came back with a teacup filled with water. He knelt beside Mallory and gave him a drink.

Mallory took big gulps, spilling it all down his neck. He stopped for air. "There was water in here the whole time?"

"Of course. A whole boiler of it. This is a steam train."

"Why would you show me kindness?"

"It's only humane to give someone water when they're thirsty."

"Always the goody-two-shoes aren't you?"

The Captain frowned and asked softly, "How do you know me?"

214

Mallory smiled a wicked, almost teasing grin. "That boy out there... you know who he is, right?"

The Captain's frown deepened. He shook his head, not understanding.

"He's dressed in overalls the colour of the sky... and so his time runs short."

Sky-blue overalls. Something in the Captain's mind *had* been stirring about it. But he couldn't figure out why.

"Hidden prophesies. Nonsense books..."

"A book..." the Captain frowned. While he wanted to know more, he wasn't comfortable finding out from Mallory, or having him on board the Train any longer. So he pushed the vague, foggy shape of a memory away for now. He allowed Evie and Paulo inside and then took the reins of Henry and Henderson. "Now, no horsing around on the Train, understand? And no manure on the carpet." He soon started the engine, and took the Train into Bethlehem.

When they arrived at Rachel's home, their shadows were long, tall giants on the ground as the sun sank low into the horizon. Rachel was thrilled to finally throw her arms around Evie to thank her for saving Daniel's life. They returned Henry and Henderson and were embraced tightly by all the

215

family members. Jared and Miriam hung themselves off Evie's legs, but they all soon had to say their goodbyes.

On their way back to the Train again, Evie asked, "Aren't you just giving Mallory what he wants by taking him away from here?"

"He can't stay here, he'll only try and conquer the world or something and mess things up. He had Violet Assassin stashed away in his stable."

"So where *are* we taking him?" Paulo asked.

The Captain paused before replying. "Back to his home. The people there can decide what to do with him."

"Which is?" Evie said.

"...Same place I'm from," he finally said.

Evie gasped and looked excited. "You mean I'm going to find out where you come from? I'm going to see your home?"

"In reply to the first statement... it would seem so," he said flatly. "And in reply to the second statement... my Train is more like home to me now. So really, you've already seen it."

Mallory glowered at them when they all stepped inside again. Evie, trying to ignore him, was eager to grab the Captain's copy of the Bible from the bookshelf and read about Jesus' birth again. She took it into the engine room and sat on the fold down driver's seat while the Captain fired up the controls.

Paulo asked, "So it was Mallory's machine that brought us here? And just today... when he tried to steal it, it came back here?"

"To three nights ago," the Captain nodded "That's why he's so grumpy. I could only set it to the time it had been in that spot before."

Evie was flicking pages madly, but looked up momentarily. "So Marius... *Mallory*, has been sitting in here for all that time? All the time we were in Bethlehem, and when I was his slave?"

"A-huh."

"So, he was in two places at once?"

"A-huh."

"But wait a minute," said Paulo. "If the Train was sitting there that whole time, why did we think it was missing in the first place?"

"Because, however his machine works, it was grabbed out of space and time as soon as we stepped out. None of the last few days had happened yet. We changed a little piece of history. It happens sometimes, you tend to get used to it."

"I still don't get it," said Evie.

"Well put it this way. If the Train were here all along, we wouldn't have had a reason to go looking for it, and so we wouldn't have ended up at

Mallory's house. Mallory wouldn't have tried to take the Train and so it couldn't have got sent back in time to land here... it's a paradox in other words."

"Time travel's nuts" Evie said, puffing out her cheeks.

The Captain cheerfully clicked a finger and pointed it at her. "That's it! Now you've got it. By the way, being back here reminds me... what else were you going to tell me that night after we'd been to the house where Jesus was?"

"Oh," Evie said, a little embarrassed. "Well, as amazing as it was holding Jesus, I was feeling guilty... you know... about my problem at school..."

"Your friend who made you cheat in the test."

"No *I* decided to cheat, and my friend found out and started blackmailing me."

"Tamara... Tonny..."

"Tanya. I've already decided to confess when I go back to school, but what I was actually feeling guilty about was the fact that I was planning how to get *her* in trouble too. Because... well, she probably won't apologise or anything."

"You want revenge."

Evie thought for a moment. She said, not proudly, "Well... yeah."

"Well I hate to tell you this, but that will only entrap you further."

"I know. I know."

"What's revenge?" asked Paulo.

Evie turned to him. "I feel bad because of her, so I want *her* to feel bad."

"Why would you want anyone to feel bad?" Paulo was utterly lost.

"Look, I know it's wrong. That's why I felt guilty. And when my tear fell on Jesus' face, I remembered the verse about Him taking our sorrows or something..."

"Surely He took up our pain and carried our sorrows..." said the Captain.

"Yeah that. Well... I guess I sort of... I don't know how to explain it..."

"We're all grasping for salvation," the Captain said. "We think we'll be free from all our bad feelings if we throw a tantrum or lash out at someone... or get revenge. You think Tanya should ask your forgiveness for wronging you. You think *she* ought to want to be 'saved', to be *freed* from her offense. But Tanya's not the one with that power. You are. She can't earn her own salvation, you have to give it. You have to forgive her."

"But she won't..."

"*Forgive* her. Just like that."

"So... forgiveness is something you do *to* someone..." Paulo said slowly, "when they've

219

treated you wrongly."

"In a nutshell, yes."

"Oooh, let's forgive Mallory!" he said excitedly.

The Captain smiled at Paulo's refreshing innocence.

"But he's not even sorry," complained Evie.

"Neither here nor there," said the Captain. "Forgiveness, salvation... *You* decide to give it. Don't wait for some scoundrel to say sorry like it's some magic password. Don't you realise how many things *you've* been forgiven for? *Without you saying sorry.* Someone has to have a huge amount of love for you to do that."

Evie tutted and rolled her eyes playfully. "Like Jesus... But *I* don't love Tanya."

"Yes you do. Well, you *can.* With help."

"It's weird."

The Captain laughed. "Weird is wonderful!" He started up the engine and once they were in flight, he reached for a string hanging from the ceiling and pulled down on it, letting out the loud steam whistle. But soon, when they landed at their destination, he was looking a lot less happy. "Come along then," he said flatly, sidling past them and walking into the carriage room. "Home sweet home, Mallory."

Mallory glanced from Paulo to the Captain, and

then slowly stood up. They all walked to the door.

The Captain stepped out onto another vast field of fresh, gleaming grass and took in a deep breath of fresh air. The others plodded down after him and looked around. Here, the glorious sunlight made each blade of grass glisten and twinkle as far as the eye could see. It was such a bright green it looked like a child's drawing. Evie and Paulo both sighed happily. But Mallory and the Captain were frowning.

"This looks *lovely* Captain!" said Evie.

"Something's wrong," he said in reply and trudged back onto the Train, while a small, scheming smile crawled onto Mallory's face.

Evie wandered a little way, enjoying the view and the sunshine. Shortly, the Captain emerged again, looking somewhat bothered and inconvenienced. "This isn't the right place."

"Of course it's the right place, it's perfect!" called out a dazed Evie.

Paulo came up to the Captain, "Did you enter in a wrong coordinate or something?"

"I'm sure I didn't. Perhaps Mallory tampered with the controls trying to get the Train to do what he wanted all the time he was stuck in there."

"Can it be fixed? I don't fancy being Mallory's travelling buddy for much longer."

The Captain looked back and forth, behind Paulo and around the field where they had landed. He saw Evie roaming around, and he saw the Train standing behind him, as he still had his glasses on, but... "Where *is* Mallory?"

Paulo's stomach dropped, his heart raced. They both quickly rushed inside the Train, but there was no sign of him there.

"Where's Mallory?" the Captain shouted to Evie. "Did you see him?"

"What? No. Haven't seen anyone."

"I took my eyes off him for a moment..." said Paulo. "I'm so sorry, Captain! He must have done a runner!"

"Well whatever this place is, he's stuck here now. He obviously preferred to take his chances here rather than back home. Let's go." On his way back to the Train, he called, "Evelyn, come on, we're going!"

There was no reply.

"Evie?" called Paulo.

They looked at each other and the Captain stepped down again from the Train to look around.

"You don't think Mallory..."

"No, look," said the Captain, relieved, but slightly perplexed. "There she is."

"What's she doing?"

Evie was walking down the hill, taking slow, even steps, holding a flower.

"I don't know. She knows not to wander off." The Captain took a step closer. "Evelyn!" he called, cupping his hands around his mouth.

She kept on walking like she was in some kind of trance.

"I'll go get her," said Paulo, jogging off down the hill.

The Captain started to follow but then something made him stop and call out, "Stop Paulo! Get away!"

A strange glow was whizzing around Evie's body. An ear-piercing screeching sound filled the air. The glow became so bright, they could no longer look, but Evie seemed unaffected. She kept walking, as though she was having a jolly Sunday stroll. Something, further down that hill, had captivated her, and it was drawing her closer and closer in...

The Carriage Room

TRAIN MANUAL

Ancient Cement
(Used by Romans)
- Quicklime (calcium oxide - heated limestone)
- Pozzolana (fine, sandy, volcanic ash)
- Pumice (volcanic rock formed when lava mixed with water — solidified rocky lav
  Cement substance created by chemical reaction

Today in the town of David, a Saviour has been born to you; He is the Messiah, the Lord.
– Luke 2:11 (NIV)

The wisemen – astronomers / astrologers
(same thing back then)
not necessarily 3 men
but 3 gifts were given.

Certain alignments of the starts and planets meant different things

Jupiter in the 'East'?   } 'New king'
Position of moon?
Alignment of three planets?

a Man who suffered, Who r pains He carried, our gs wrong with us... it was d tore and crushed Him – our sins!

He took the punishment hrough His bruises we get healed.
– Isaiah 53:2-5 (MSG)

Herod the Great Jewish 'client' king under the rule of Roman Empire

Famous for architecture and building projects rebuilt the Temple of Jerusalem but brutal and ruthless

'Valeo' – Latin expression of farewell

TRAIN FLIGHT

THE SANCTUARY

Need a holiday?

This
Newton' documenting our movements?
Do I know her in
my future?
"a happened on Planet Zero...

TWO
dimensions occupying
the same space...

Investigate aligning orientation
mismatch between dimensions

Did Mallory get stuck there?

DIMENSIONALLY VER

ABOUT ELIZABETH NEWTON

Elizabeth Newton appears to have a very ordinary life. She currently cannot travel in space and time, except of course in the conventional way. The same way *you* do when walking across a room and moving through your day minute by minute. She also hasn't had much experience with travelling to the Middle East, but she does read a lot. And reading, as you should know by now, is basically a window to anywhere. *But it's not like actually being there,* I hear you say. And you're right. But it certainly has got to be the next best thing. (And the cost of a book is considerably cheaper than plane tickets.)

Anyway, she also has never been covered in cement, luckily, or made to wash someone's feet. She *has* washed a number of feet in her time, out of choice. And she *has* been forgiven for many things, without her having said sorry. She has regularly fought off the urge to 'get revenge'. It certainly is hard to do, but the trick is to remember that this isn't Serothia, and nobody's perfect.

Elizabeth has many jobs in her life, from washing dishes to marking maths tests, from organising church rosters to picking up dirty socks. Writing stories is her way of having exciting adventures, and in some ways it's better than doing the actual adventures because you can more easily drink a cup of tea while doing it.

www.facebook.com/trainflight | trainflightbooks@gmail.com

HAVE ALL THE ADVENTURES!

Season One - Books 1 - 5!

#1 Moon Man

#2 The Birth of Salvation

#3 The Sanctuary

#4 Furry Friends

#5 The End of the Night

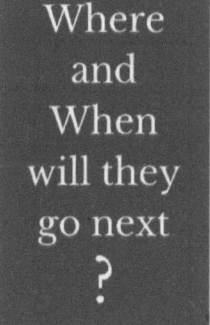

Look out for Season 2!